HEARTS AND CRAFTS

Eduardo Noriega struggles financially with running the family estate in Spain. He's also responsible for the farm, his mother and Maria, a family servant. When some furniture is in need of urgent renovation friends recommend Claire, who travels to Casona de la Esquina from England — despite the expense involved. Her arrival upsets Elena, a neighbour's daughter, who imagined waltzing down the aisle with Eduardo. Claire does her job, uncovers an intriguing family secret . . . and changes everyone's plans, including her own.

Books by Wendy Kremer
in the Linford Romance Library:

REAP THE WHIRLWIND
AT THE END OF THE RAINBOW
WHERE THE BLUEBELLS GROW WILD
WHEN WORDS GET IN THE WAY
COTTAGE IN THE COUNTRY
WAITING FOR A STAR TO FALL
SWINGS AND ROUNDABOUTS
KNAVE OF DIAMONDS
SPADES AND HEARTS
TAKING STEPS
I'LL BE WAITING

WENDY KREMER

HEARTS AND CRAFTS

Complete and Unabridged

LINFORD
Leicester

First published in Great Britain in 2011

First Linford Edition
published 2013

British Library CIP Data

Kremer, Wendy.
Hearts and crafts. - -
(Linford romance library)
1. Love stories.
2. Large type books.
I. Title II. Series
823.9′2–dc23

ISBN 978–1–4448–1469–9

Published by
F. A. Thorpe (Publishing)
Anstey, Leicestershire

Set by Words & Graphics Ltd.
Anstey, Leicestershire
Printed and bound in Great Britain by
T. J. International Ltd., Padstow, Cornwall

This book is printed on acid-free paper

1

Claire left the visitor to her small antique shop alone for a few minutes, so that he could browse at leisure before she approached him. Some people didn't want to be spoken to at all. She usually made a tentative approach if she noticed someone was showing obvious interest. When he glanced in her direction, she left her desk, strolled over to him, and asked, 'Can I help?'

He had a deep voice with a slight accent. 'Perhaps. We have a mutual friend, and he recommended I drop in and have a word with you.'

Intrigued, Claire gave a hesitant smile. 'A mutual friend?'

He was very tall; his head almost touched the low-beamed ceiling. The small windowpanes allowed little day-light into the display room; she could tell he had jet-black hair but not whether his eyes were black or brown, though they were very dark. His clothes looked expensive, and he gave the impression he was someone who knew what he wanted and had enough confidence to get it. There was no hesitation in his expression; it was serious and decisive. He looked down at her pale face and gave her the information she'd asked for. 'David . . . David Willows?'

'Yes, David is a good friend. What can I do for you, Mr . . . ?'

He held out his hand. 'Eduardo Noriega. David and I went to the same boarding school, and we've kept in touch.'

She nodded and felt a little nervous as she accepted his hand. As far as she could recall neither David, nor David's wife, Susan, had ever mentioned this man's name, but she didn't doubt he was telling the truth.

He continued to explain. 'I've some pieces of English furniture that need restoring and David recommended you.' He looked around and gestured. 'Did you restore all of this?'

'No, not everything. Some of the items are on commission, I've restored others, and a couple were in such good condition they didn't need any help.' She smiled. 'There are occasions when restoration can actually reduce the value of something.'

'Which items have you restored?' His eyes were probing.

She turned away and moved ahead of him towards a shiny table in the bow-shaped window. She placed her hands on the back of a dining chair. 'For example, these. I bought three mahogany dining-chairs in very good condition, apart from the upholstery, a couple of years ago at an auction and searched in vain for others to complete the set. In the end I added another three, the same age and a similar design although they were badly damaged. The front legs have slightly different carved detailing.'

He crouched down and nodded. 'I see what you mean. But the legs will spend most of their lives under the table anyway, so no one will notice the difference, will they?' He stood up; his height and physical presence captured Claire's whole attention.

She had to strive to concentrate on her job. 'Exactly. This balloon-backed style was popular throughout the nineteenth century. The original three chairs were in good condition and just needed re-upholstering.

'The ones I found later needed stripping and cleaning, their joints strengthening, and the supporting webbing had collapsed, so the entire seating structure needed reworking before I could re-upholster them in the matching velvet. I'm more than happy with the results, however, and the full set is already sold. Their new owner will be picking them up this weekend.'

He gave her the mere ghost of a smile. His white teeth glistened briefly in a face that was tanned and clearly continental. 'The furniture I have is larger, but I can see why David recommended you.'

'What are we talking about, exactly?'

'A chest of drawers, a leather-topped desk, and a three-piece desk suite. They were excellent pieces once, but now they have damaged joints and peeling veneer. The chest's drawers are difficult to open and they all have stains and scratches. There's an antique pine wardrobe, too; in excellent condition outwardly, but one of the legs is damaged. I've brought some photos.'

He reached into the inner pocket of his soft overcoat and handed her a pouch with pictures.

She shuffled through them and gave them a knowledgeable scrutiny. 'I see what you mean. I presume you want an estimate of what I'd charge to restore them. I'm sure you realise it's very hard, if not impossible, for me to guess by simply looking at photos. I'd need to actually see them and examine them before I can make an educated guess.'

'That's a problem; you see, I live in Spain.'

Trying not to look disappointed, she responded, 'Oh — then it'd be more sensible for you to look for someone local to do the job.' Hoping still, because she needed the work, she added, 'If you want me to handle it, I could arrange to have them transported here and back to you again, but that would add significantly to the cost.' Curiosity made her ask, 'Isn't there anyone qualified living somewhere nearby?'

'No one who specialises in English furniture. The pieces came to Spain with my grandmother when she married my grandfather. They meant a great deal to her because they were a link to her homeland for as long as she lived. She made us promise never to sell them, or to let them out of the house. I want to save them before it's too late, even though it's probably a costly undertaking.

'After Gran's death, they were left in an outlying cottage for years, and no one realised how much damage damp and neglect could do. It was almost too late by the time we moved them back to the barn. But once they're repaired, we'll take more care of them, in the main house.'

Her grey eyes were interested; she handed the pictures back.

He accepted them from her and continued, 'David said you might be glad of a commission. He said you're good at what you do and that you have an excellent reputation. I need a good craftsman who knows about English furniture. It would be a satisfactory arrangement for us both.'

Claire coloured slightly and hoped David hadn't made it sound as if she was desperate for work — even if it was close to the truth.

'I'm so sorry, Mr Noriega, but I don't really see how I can help since I'm here and the furniture is in Spain.'

'I wondered if you'd be able to come

to Spain and work on the furniture . . . ?'

'You want me to come to Spain?' Her surprise couldn't have been greater and it showed in her expression.

He nodded. 'We have plenty of space and you can work at your own pace. Why not come and make your estimate to begin with?' he continued. 'Then if we both decide it's a viable undertaking, you can either start right away, or come back later, as you wish.'

Claire ran her hand through her auburn hair, ruffling her wealth of curls. She thought about the idea and was tempted. She didn't have any commissions at present, and there were none on the horizon either. She could fill in time restoring other furniture she'd bought cheaply at auctions, but that wouldn't improve her immediate finances. Shop and internet deals were always unpredictable. The sale of the dining chairs on Saturday would pacify her bank manager for a while, but for how long?

She met Eduardo Noriega's eyes, and something about him made her consider the idea seriously; she liked his direct and down-to-earth manner. She had the feeling it was a task she might enjoy; it sounded like an unusual and interesting job.

'I'll have to think about it. I have my shop to consider; I can't just close it for an indefinite period. And I really can't give you a rough guess about costs until I've examined the furniture. What if I travel out there and the estimate turns out to be more than you expect?'

'I'm presuming that you'll be able to restore at least some of the pieces before the costs outrun my fantasies.' He smiled cautiously. 'I do understand that it all depends on what you find, and that you can't decide here and now.'

He took a visiting card out of his wallet and handed it to her with the photos again. 'I'll leave you my phone number and the photos. I'm in the UK until the weekend. I'd be grateful if you could decide one way or the other and let me know.'

Holding the embossed card and the envelope tightly, she nodded. 'Yes, of course. I just need a day or two to consider things carefully.'

'Good.' He looked around apprais-ingly. 'It's a nice little shop, by the way, but a pity that it's tucked away down a side-street. Otherwise I'm sure you'd be overrun with customers.' He held out his hand.

Claire took it; his handshake was warm and firm. 'Yes — but if we were closer to the main road, the rent would be higher and the quiet side-street atmosphere would be lost. People who like antiques like to wander where it's peaceful and quiet.'

With an answering smile, he nodded understandingly and looked around the shop again before he turned away. The old-fashioned bell over the doorframe tinkled as he opened the door. Ducking under the lintel, he looked back and lifted his hand silently before shutting the door behind him and striding off briskly down the street.

From the window, Claire noticed how he yanked up the collar of his coat. Evidently, the English springtime temperatures were cooler than Spanish ones. His black hair glistened in the sunlight and Claire still wondered whether his eyes were brown or black.

She tapped the visiting card in her hand and turned towards her workshop in the rear. Smiling to herself, she mused that if David knew him, then he wasn't a serial killer trying to lure her into a trap. It was a serious proposition.

She propped his card prominently on the desk and left the envelope with the photos next to it.

She put on a long working overall to protect her clothes. It was counter-productive to appear in stained clothes in the display room if someone was thinking about buying an expensive item of furniture.

She picked up a mortise chisel and mallet to take out a joint on an upholstered chair she was repairing for a friend of her mother's. Someone who, yet again, seemed to think Claire could live on water and fresh air.

She knew she ought to refuse this kind of job, but they always talked her round as soon as they began telling her what a lovely person her mother was.

* * *

A couple of weeks later, Claire had managed to make arrangements and was on her way to Spain. Her mother had reluctantly agreed to move into Claire's small flat and run the shop until her return. Claire's assurances that Bill, her next-door neighbour, only needed a bang on the wall to come running if there was any kind of problem tipped the scales.

Bill was a love; he helped her to move things around in the shop, unloaded and loaded furniture for her, and even took over in the shop in an emergency. He was a jovial, pleasant man with a round face and a tidy beard. She'd left a couple of items of replacement furniture ready, too, in case they managed to sell something in her absence. Claire was quite sure the shop would be in safe hands until her return.

Eduardo Noriega's suggestion that she could fly over and hire a car at the airport was swept aside when she explained it'd be a waste of time to make multiple journeys back and forth; if they could agree on the cost of the repairs, she'd begin working straight away.

She'd load her Jeep straight off with her tools, pieces of spare wood and various other items she thought she might need. Having a car wasn't important, but having her tools and equipment was. He agreed, and transferred the money for the ferry to her account a few days later. Claire now only hoped they could agree on a price, and that she'd make enough profit from the job to shut the bank manager up for a bit.

She drove to Portsmouth and caught the ferry to Santander.

The ferry took almost twenty-four hours. She enjoyed the trip, and had a good night's sleep before it finally sailed into Santander early the following afternoon. The sun was shining and there was a pleasant fragrance of salty water, grasses and herbage in the sea breezes as she waited for the ship to dock. She needed a lightweight jacket to keep out the cool air, but it still felt almost like going on holiday.

Once she was out of the port, she pulled into the side of the road and fed into her GPS system the address Mr Noriega had given her.

She adjusted to the flow of traffic and headed out of Santander. Claire left the thinking up to her GPS system and relaxed. After a while, it directed her along some country roads and then instructed her to turn off onto a side road, announcing that Casona de la Esquina was two kilometres further on.

The area was quiet, hilly, green and

rural. Claire was pleasantly surprised. She had a picture of sun-drenched landscapes whenever she thought of Spain; this part of the country wasn't like that at all. The road ran past well-nurtured pastures and grazing cattle and ended eventually in front of a substantial building of rough stone, and a collection of outhouses. She parked the Jeep, got out and stretched.

In front of the large, sprawling house was a paved courtyard with decorative stonework. A wooden bench stood next to the entrance. The austere effect of rough walls was softened by occasional containers filled with bright red flowers. Looking up, she studied the dark balcony running the length of the upper level. The house had an overhanging roof and the woodwork was beautifully carved; Claire realised that it would provide welcome shade and cooler temperatures in the upper rooms on a sunny summer day.

Claire used the old-fashioned knocker

and soon heard the shuffle of footsteps echoing on the floor from within. The door opened to reveal an older woman in an old-fashioned wrap-around apron. She was short, with slightly rounded shoulders and grey hair drawn back into a severe bun. Her black eyes twinkled in a bronzed and lined complexion.

Claire hoped she understood English. 'Good afternoon. My name is Claire Coleman. Mr Noriega is expecting me.'

The woman nodded and gave her a toothy smile. 'Yes, we are expecting you. Eduardo is out in the fields, but he'll be back soon. Come in. I expect you would like some tea.'

Claire beamed; the woman spoke good English and there was the welcome prospect of a cup of tea. 'That would be lovely. Thank you.'

The woman opened the heavy door further; it swung open easily. She stood aside and added, 'I am Maria. I will take you to Señora Noriega and then make the tea.'

Following her, Claire observed, 'You

speak such good English. Where did you learn?'

Evidently flattered, Maria explained, 'I came to work in the house when I was a young girl. Eduardo's grandmother was alive in those days and I asked her to teach me. We all speak English. Eduardo's mother kept up the tradition; Eduardo and his sister went to boarding school in England for a couple of years and the next generation of children already speak English too.'

Claire passed through a large, flagged hallway with rough stone walls. It was sparsely furnished with some heavy Spanish pieces. A winding staircase led upwards to a gallery with a carved railing. Apart from some central heating radiators, nothing had been changed for centuries.

Maria opened a heavy door into a large room with a dark-beamed ceiling. A woman with salt-and-pepper hair was sitting in an armchair looking out across a north-facing patio. Beyond it, through the French windows, Claire glimpsed an expanse of countryside, and some mountains in the far distance.

With a welcoming expression, the older woman stood up. She was of middling height, had a good figure and a pleasant face. Her hair was drawn back by two decorative clips and she was wearing a white blouse and black trousers. She came forward, her hand outstretched.

'You must be Miss Coleman.'

Claire took it and nodded. 'Please, call me Claire.'

'Eduardo said you'd be arriving today. Did you have a good journey?'

'Yes, thank you. I was told it can be a rough crossing, but it was fine.'

'The Bay of Biscay is sometimes stormy, but it's not so bad at this time of year. Please, sit down.'

Claire did as she was asked and settled in a comfortable armchair facing Mrs Noriega. She noticed that Maria had discreetly left the room and was probably getting the tea. Her glance was captivated by an ancient wood-burning fireplace set among the stonework along one wall. It dominated the room. 'What a magnificent fireplace,' she remarked. 'This house is very old, isn't it?'

Mrs Noriega gazed at the silent, empty fireplace. 'I must admit I love that fireplace. In past times, it was probably the main source of heat and an essential necessity. We still use it now and then in winter; nothing is as cosy as a real fire, is it? Yes, you're right,' she continued. 'The house is old, although there are older ones in the area. It is typical for this region. We've modernised it to make it more comfortable, but the basic structure hasn't changed much since it was built.

'The farmhouse was once the centre of a large estate; it's been in the family since the eighteenth century. A lot of the land has been sold off and Eduardo is doing his best to hang on to what's left.'

'Farmhouse? That's an understatement — it's more like a manor house, or a country residence.'

Mrs Noriega laughed softly. 'It's a family home; a farmhouse that has expanded with time.'

Maria returned with a tray and proceeded to hand around teacups and offer some cake. Claire noticed that she'd removed her apron and calmly joined them, so she wasn't a menial housekeeper; more a family friend.

Claire took a sip of tea. 'I love the rough stonework everywhere. I admire you for resisting the lure of changing it radically, even though it's sometimes easier to give into modern temptations.'

'People around this region cling to what they have, I suppose. People living in towns and cities have completely different needs and rhythms.'

Claire nodded. 'And of course very country, every region develops its own style and appearance, usually influenced by the kind of materials that happen to be available locally.'

'True,' Mrs Noriega agreed. 'There was an abundance of forests around here in the past and that's probably why there is so much woodwork and so many balconies in the older houses. It was cheap and available. The forests had almost disappeared, but the authorities have been trying to re-cultivate them for decades; it's a slow job. Materials like flagstones or rough brickwork are not very practical, or very comfortable these days, so most people have replaced them with labour-saving surfaces. But no one in our family seems to have wanted to change things much, apart from adding the occasional extension. Perhaps there was just never enough money when someone considered changing something — or we were just too lazy.'

She smiled briefly again. 'Apart from electricity, central heating and modern windows, we've left our home as it was.' She placed her cup on the small side table. 'I think Eduardo has explained why he wants my mother's furniture restored on-the-spot? He told us you're a trained restorer. It's an unusual profession for a woman, isn't it?'

'Yes, he told me why. It isn't such an unusual job for a woman these days. I know of a few others. I did my apprenticeship with a very good restorer and spent two years with a carpenter learning some of his trade.'

'And you like your work?'

'I love it. I was always fascinated by old furniture and it's very rewarding to restore damaged items to their former glory.'

'Well, I'm glad you're here and I hope you can save my mother's furniture for us. It's been neglected for too long, but money was needed for other investments to keep the farm going. Eduardo has been hoping to draw off enough money to do the repairs for some time.

'The cottage where nearly all the furniture stood was my mother's retreat. No one used it after her death, and no one realised the effect damp would have on the furniture. We should have had more sense, and lit fires regularly to keep the damp at bay.' She sighed, then added, 'Eduardo was extremely fond of my mother, and she of him. He feels obligated to fulfil the family's promise to look after her furniture. Pablo and Eduardo have already transferred it all into the barn. One item, a pine wardrobe, is here in one of the bedrooms. It's always been there, but I don't think it needs quite as much attention as the other things.'

There was a sound of firm footsteps on the flagstones in the hall. When Eduardo Noriega entered the room, Claire's awareness of all her senses soared a few notches.

He was just as she remembered him. He was an extremely attractive man with a ruggedly handsome face and a special aura; his looks impressed her. It didn't lessen his attraction that today he was dressed in washed-out jeans that hugged his slim hips and a working shirt that pulled across his broad shoulders.

He pulled off leather working gloves and bundled them into one hand. His expression was conventional but welcoming. 'Hello. You made it then — without any problems I hope?' She nodded. 'I saw your Jeep and thought I'd come to greet you and show you the items you've come to save — and where you'll be staying.'

Claire nodded. She could at last ascertain that his eyes were the colour of dark chocolate. She studied the lean, tanned face, the black hair gleaming in the light; she liked what she saw.

His mother answered impatiently, 'Eduardo, she's only just arrived. Give her a chance to finish her tea.'

He smiled at his mother and Claire could tell they got on well.

'As you can see, Mother, I don't have a whip in my hand and I'd no intention of parting her from her tea cup.' His tone was smooth but there was amusement in his eyes.

Claire put the delicate cup back into its saucer and stood up. 'That's perfectly okay. I'm here to do a job.' She got up. 'Thank you for the tea; it was just what I needed.'

Mrs Noriega replied, 'You're very welcome.' Eyeing her son with amusement, she added darkly, 'Don't let Eduardo bully you into working today.'

Claire laughed softly. 'If we agree on a price, the time I need to complete the job is up to me. The sooner I start, the sooner I finish, and the sooner I can get out from underneath everyone's feet again.'

Claire smiled at her hostess, and hastened to catch up with Eduardo who was already on his way out.

As she watched the young woman hurrying after her son, Sophia Noriega decided she was a nice girl. She was pretty, with a slim figure, oval face and quiet grey eyes. Her rich auburn hair was a lovely colour and cut in a neat bob. She had a generous smile, was a modern, trained specialist and as polite as most English people were. She seemed the type of girl who wouldn't cause much disruption to the daily routine of the farm or the household.

Eduardo paused at the front door, holding it open. Claire sidled through the narrow space past him, then kept pace as he moved towards one of the outhouses to the side of the big house. On the way, he asked politely about her journey.

He paused in front of what had probably once been a storage shed or a barn. The old entrance doors had been replaced by modern ones with an upper section of windowpanes. She followed him inside and was immediately impressed by the size of the place.

He indicated towards the table tennis equipment on one side; the corner of his mouth curled. 'I hope you don't mind that being there. I don't think it'll get in your way. The children play now and again, and I didn't have anywhere else to put it. I think you still have enough room for your work.'

Claire felt a lungful of disappointment. Eduardo was the only young person she'd met, so logically the children were his. When she'd phoned David to ask about Eduardo, David had merely commented that he was a nice chap and ran a farm. David didn't reveal any personal details and she hadn't wanted to appear too inquisitive.

Claire looked around. 'No, there's plenty of room. A lot more than in my own workshop. If I need things to be dust-free for a few hours, I'm sure I can organise things so that the children aren't around just then. It's ideal; clean, light and airy, and ample room for me to move around.'

'If you open the doors, you'll have more light. It's quite mild.'

She nodded. 'A little warmer than in the UK.' She spotted the furniture in the shadows, lined up against the rear wall. 'That's it?'

'Yes, please take a look at your leisure. I don't expect a verdict here and now. My mother was right when she said you need time to settle in.' He stuck one hand in his pocket. His shirt strained in all the right places and Claire decided that, married or not, Eduardo was an attention-grabbing man.

'Come with me. I'll show you where I thought you might like to stay. You're welcome to stay with us in the house if you prefer, of course, but I thought you might like some privacy and freedom. We have a small, self-contained cottage that my sister uses whenever she's at home. I thought you might like it too.'

Claire was intrigued — it sounded ideal. They seemed to be very friendly people, but she was a stranger, employed by them, and it might become a strain to share in their daily routine for a couple of weeks. She longed to stop and examine the furniture, but hurried after him instead.

He went ahead around the corner towards another building. It had a couple of up-and-down small windows and a bright green painted door. 'This used to be a pigsty,' he explained. 'But we gave up breeding pigs years ago.'

Her nose wrinkled as a picture of grunting, mud-encrusted pigs drifted across her imagination.

He went on, 'My sister had the idea of making holiday homes as an additional source of income, but it never really took off because we're too far from the coast and this area isn't well known to tourists.' He flung open the door and motioned her inside. 'It wasn't completely in vain, though, because she now has her own little kingdom when she and her husband come back for a visit.'

Claire went ahead and looked around. The size and shape reminded her vaguely of her own shop. The ceiling was low-beamed with old timbers, the furniture highly polished and good quality. There was a small half-hidden alcove harbouring a small kitchen unit. The walls were white-washed and uneven. Floral curtains fluttered at the open window and someone had put some wild flowers in a terracotta vase on the windowsill.

She smiled. 'It looks lovely.'

'There are two small bedrooms upstairs. One is bigger than the other one. You can take your pick — that's if you'd like to stay here, of course.' He gave her a lop-sided smile and her stomach flipped. Claire was rational enough to know it was a stupid reaction about someone who was practically a stranger — and married into the bargain.

'I'd love to stay here, if you'll let me,' she said.

'Good, that's settled then. If you make your own breakfast, you are independent of us and can start whatever time you like. Or you can come across for breakfast if you prefer. Either way, Maria will supply you with whatever you need. She makes something at lunchtime to keep us going, but we have our main meal in the evening and we'd like you to join us for that. Usually about eight-thirty to nine pm. Maria enjoys cooking and she'll love the chance to show off a bit.'

'I like cooking too, but I don't usually have much time to do so until the shop closes, so I'm already used to main evening meals. Your plan would suit me fine. Are you sure no one will mind having a stranger sitting at the dining table for a while?'

'No, Maria will probably be extremely offended if you don't come. You can scuttle off again afterwards — or not, according to how you feel.'

'Well, as long as I don't disturb your daily life too much, I'll accept gratefully. It will leave me free to concentrate on the work and that means I'll need less time.'

'Good, that's settled then. I'll help you with your luggage before I disappear back to work.'

She studied his features. 'Most of the stuff in the Jeep is working equipment. I only have one suitcase, and I can manage that on my own.'

His eyebrows lifted, the corner of his mouth went up and his dark eyes twinkled. 'One suitcase? I thought women always went around with a portable wardrobe in tow.'

'One suitcase is all I need at the moment. I'm not expecting to attend many social affairs. I'm here to work. I always try not to rely on male help unless I know something is very heavy.'

'Well, what about your tools?'

'If you help me with the heavier pieces of wood, I'll be grateful, but it's not absolutely necessary either. I'm used to managing. My tools are mostly old-fashioned and portable. Apart from things like a sander or a drill, I don't use much electric equipment.'

He eyed her thoughtfully. 'Well, let's get your bits of wood into the barn, then I'll leave you to unpack and sort out the rest of your stuff. We'll meet up again for dinner. Just come across when you're ready.'

She nodded and followed him out of her temporary abode.

After stacking some pieces of wood for her, he went back to whatever he was doing before she arrived.

She dragged her suitcase into the house and took it upstairs before going back to the Jeep to unload the other tools, the veneers, and all the other various items she'd brought with her. She forced herself to ignore the furniture. She'd make a careful examination tomorrow. It was too late to do much today; the afternoon was already on the wane. She arranged her equipment in a tidy row on a dilapidated but solid-looking worktable ranged along the wall. All the prerequisites for her to do a good job were there. She drove the Jeep round and parked it out of the way alongside her new temporary home.

About to go inside, she heard children's voices. They were strolling down the lane behind her house and going towards the main house. The boy was scuffing the ground, kicking up loose dirt and looking grim.

Claire smiled at the little girl and got a shy smile in return.

Claire ventured, 'Hello.'

Evidently glad of a diversion, the child replied, 'Hello . . . who are you?'

Extremely pretty, her black hair was tied back in a bright blue ribbon; it cascaded to her shoulders and shone in the sunlight. Long black lashes framed dark-blue eyes in a face with an even olive complexion. Her brother was dark, too. He was older, taller, with bold, questioning eyes. His expression told Claire that he thought unfamiliar women were a pain in the neck.

'I'm Claire. I've come to repair some furniture.'

'I'm Alisa and this is my brother, Antonio.' She tilted her head to the side and she looked at Claire with a puzzled expression. 'But you're a woman. Do women repair furniture?'

'Of course. Why not? Women can do most things men do, especially when they've had proper training.'

'Don't ask silly questions, Alisa. It's not important. Let's go and see the donkey.' He reminded Claire of Eduardo; the same dark eyes, high cheekbones and strong chin.

Alisa's lips pouted and she bravely stood her own ground. 'I am not silly,' she scolded. 'And you can't boss me around! You pretend to know everything better, but you don't.'

Claire felt sorry for them; they were obviously bored.

In a squeaky voice, Alisa explained, 'We want to go to the pond to see the ducks, but we're not allowed to go on our own.'

Claire thought briefly about her unopened suitcase. She liked children. 'How about me? I'll come with you, if you get permission. I'd like to see your pond. I've just arrived, and I'd like to see a little more of where I'll be staying for a while.'

Alisa clapped her hands. 'Really? Come on, Antonio, let's ask Gran.'

Antonio grinned at Claire, all his former reservations forgotten. 'That would be great!'

Antonio led the way, a few steps ahead of Alisa and Claire. The little girl skipped alongside Claire, chattering. She clutched a paper bag filled with stale bread, explaining, 'I have a favourite duck. It always comes to me as soon as I arrive.'

Claire smiled. 'I'm sure it does; especially if you bring it bread. It's clearly an intelligent duck.'

Alisa giggled.

Claire liked the hilly contours of the landscape. The children led her up a gentle incline covered with rough grass and low bushes and when they reached the top, she could see a lot more of the surrounding countryside. It was approaching sunset and the light was very beautiful. Red and orange splashes of sunlight spread their fingers across the straggling scenery; the air was clean and sharp.

The soothing silence was broken by the sound of hoof beats and a man on a big horse hurtled up the slope towards them. The rider, in jodhpurs and a white shirt, looked completely at ease astride a black stallion. When he drew alongside, he reined in and studied them all.

His glance lingered on Claire and he threw a leg over the saddle before jumping down.

Claire stood her ground and waited. He was almost as tall as Eduardo. His hair was just as black, but not cut as neatly and it reached the collar of his stylish shirt. He had brown eyes and dazzling white teeth in a tanned face. He said something to the children in Spanish, and they evidently explained who she was.

He made an extravagant bow and his eyes swept over her appreciatively, casting an approving glance at her shapely figure in blue jeans and indigo T-shirt. He was an extremely attractive male, but there was something about him that made Claire feel cautious. She couldn't define what bothered her; perhaps it was the way the dark eyes narrowed and studied her like a hawk. Perhaps it was his proud, almost arrogant bearing. Perhaps she was just being silly.

He held out his hand with long, tapering fingers and Claire accepted it.

'Hello. I'm Juan De Silva, from the neighbouring farm over there.' He tipped his head in the appropriate direction.

He held her hand too long and that didn't help to lessen her misgivings, although she kept her voice light and level when she replied, 'Hello, I'm Claire Coleman. I'm here to work on some furniture for Eduardo Noriega.'

She freed herself of his grip as unobtrusively as she could. Ill at ease with him, she looked away for a moment towards a small cottage down in the hollow of a neighbouring field. The bright sun was sinking behind the horizon; colourful reds and golds reflected from the windows and flashed like living flames. When she looked up at Juan De Silva again, for a moment, his figure seemed a dark silhouette surrounded by the blazing shades of the sunset. Goose pimples covered her arms, even though the day was still warm.

'Hi Claire, nice to meet you. Where are you going?' His voice was deep and his English was excellent.

Claire speculated that he seemed to be one of those men who simply brimmed with self-confidence in the presence of strange women. He showed no sign of cagey politeness. As her Mum would say, he was a smooth operator.

She answered politely, 'The children are taking me to their pond to feed the ducks. They're showing me around the place as I've only just arrived.'

He nodded. 'Such a pity. If I didn't have a previous appointment, I'd love to come with you and we could get to know each other better.' He gave Claire a brilliant smile. 'Still, we are sure to meet again. I hope you enjoy your stay — and don't let Eduardo work you too hard. You must pay us a visit us one day. I'll look forward to seeing you again.'

He ruffled Antonio's head, murmured something in Spanish to the two children and leaped up elegantly into the saddle again. 'Bye, you two. Bye, Claire. See you very soon, I hope.'

Claire managed to sound as perfectly at ease as she answered, 'Goodbye, and it was nice to meet you.'

He tipped his whip to his forehead before he gave his stallion the order to move and galloped off in the direction of the Noriega farm without a backward glance.

Claire felt almost relieved to be on her own with the children again. The sun had moved behind some trees and reduced the colours mirrored in the cottage windows. It looked almost like any other old cottage now. She turned her attention to the two children. 'So, where's your pond?'

Alisa pointed down the hill to a nearby grove of trees in a neighbouring field to the cottage. Claire understood why Señora Noriega didn't want them to go there on their own. It was a solitary place, hidden from the farm-house and out of earshot.

She followed them until they reached the edge of the water. 'You both speak such good English. Where did you learn?'

'In school, and from our mum. We go to international schools that teach everything in English.'

'Really? Is there an international school near here?'

'No, I don't think so. We're only going to the local school until Mum gets back. It's hard to make real friends here, though because we're not near the village and the others know we'll be leaving soon.'

Puzzled, Claire decided not to ask any more questions in case there was some kind of family conflict in progress. The children didn't seem bothered that their mother was somewhere else. Perhaps there was a simple explanation.

Claire watched the children feeding the ducks, and then they began skimming stones across the water. Antonio was more successful and, however much Alisa tried, she couldn't manage more than two skips.

Claire comforted her by saying, 'I was never very good at that kind of thing either, Alisa. Some of us are good at this and others are good at that, but no one is good at everything.'

Alisa nodded in agreement but kept on trying.

By the time they returned home, Claire already liked the two children. They were all hungry and they parted company at her temporary abode.

She had time to unpack her suitcase and freshen up before she went across for the evening meal. When she did, daylight had almost faded and she was glad she wore a cardigan over her T-shirt. She presumed that she was suitably dressed. If they expected her to change for dinner, they'd be disappointed. Her present wardrobe was too meagre for that.

She knocked on the front door and

Maria came to let her in.

'Come around the back to the kitchen from now on,' she told Claire. 'We eat there when there are no guests. Eduardo should have told you. The back door is always open.' Bustling ahead of her, Maria added warmly, 'We don't classify you as a guest.'

Claire relaxed. 'That's good,' she said.

The kitchen was roomy and lived-in. There was an over-large kitchen table covered in a blue and white checked tablecloth. A terracotta pottery vase on the windowsill was filled with the same wild flowers as in her own cottage. The table was set for four, although there was room for twelve. A collection of shiny pots and kitchen utensils hung from the walls near a big cooking stove. On it, saucepans were already bubbling away, sending forth delicious odours. Onions, peppers, dried tomatoes and garlic hung in long strips from hooks in the ceiling. Claire hoped no one could hear her stomach rumbling.

Mrs Noriega looked up when Claire came in. She was arranging some dishes on the table. 'Ah, good! Eduardo will be with us in a minute, he's just washing his hands. Sit down, Claire; it doesn't matter where. No one has a special place.'

'Thanks. Can I help?'

She smiled. 'Thank you, but no. Maria doesn't like anyone interfering in her kitchen, do you, Maria? I think there'd be a war if anyone tried.'

Maria headed for the pots on the stove, looking complacent. 'I like cooking and it's my job in this house. If I need help, then I'm not doing my job properly.'

Claire's smile flashed understandingly. She looked at the place settings. 'What about the children?'

'They've eaten, and are already in bed. Probably not sleeping — they always read a bit before they fall asleep. I'll check on them later,' Mrs Noriega explained. 'They start school early, and need plenty of sleep. They eat with us at the weekend when sleep is not so important.'

'They're a lively pair. Eduardo must be very proud of them. They speak such good English and they're very polite.'

Sophia Noriega looked up with a puzzled expression. 'Eduardo? You sound like you think Eduardo should be more proud of them than us.'

Claire coloured slightly. 'Oh . . . I assumed they were his children. They told me their mother would be back in a couple of weeks, and I'm afraid I just presumed . . . '

Maria hooted. 'Eduardo — a father? I've been waiting for that day for thirty-three years! I wish he'd get on with it, so that I see his children before I die.'

Mrs Noriega smiled and explained, 'Antonio and Alisa are my daughter's children. Her husband is in the diplomatic corps and they're constantly on the move. Usually the children go to school wherever Javier is posted. At present, it's Moldavia and Christina wasn't happy with the standard so she decided to send them home for the last couple of months. A friend accompanied them to London, and Eduardo collected them and brought them home. It looks as if Javier will probably be posted to Washington next time, so there'll be no problem about schooling there.'

'And the children don't miss their parents?'

'No doubt they do, in their own way, but they talk to them at least once a day via . . . what's the name of it . . . skite or something similar?'

Claire said helpfully, 'Skype?'

'Yes that's it. It's wonderful. They sit in front of the computer and talk to their parents thousands of miles away. We don't need to do anything — they know exactly what to do. Eduardo uses the computer all the time, but I've never been interested enough to bother. The nearest I ever get to computers is fetching cash from the automatic teller.'

'I use my computer for my job,'

Claire said. 'The internet is important as a selling platform, and for keeping in touch. I'm sure Alisa and Antonio feel happier when they can see and talk to their parents every day.'

'Yes, and they take it all for granted.'

Just then Eduardo came in, his shirt sleeves rolled up and smelling of sandalwood soap. Claire was thankful that everything was so informal. She told herself she was merely pleased because things were so homely and it had nothing at all to do with the fact that Eduardo Noriega wasn't married.

Maria began to serve out the steaming, fragrant food. When she looked at Eduardo, she began to chortle.

Pulling out his chair, he looked at her and asked benignly, 'What's the joke then, Maria?'

'Did you realise you had two children?'

Startled, he replied, 'Pardon?'

'Claire thought Antonio and Alisa were yours.'

He looked at Claire briefly, his dark brows lifted but he was clearly amused. 'If no one, including me, explained who they are and why they're here, then that's very understandable.'

Handing him a bowl of steaming vegetables, Maria said, 'It's about time you had some children of your own.'

Sophia Noriega was torn between gravity and laughter. 'Maria, don't start all that again.'

Eduardo picked up his knife and fork. 'When I want children, you'll be the first to know.'

Maria cackled with laughter. 'But not before you've settled things with your wife, I would hope.'

His eyebrows rose in amusement again but he didn't reply. It was clearly a recurring topic and he chose not to pursue it further. He busied himself with his plate instead.

Claire picked up her cutlery and tried not to deliberate too much about the dark man sitting opposite.

She enjoyed being with the family

and they made an effort to speak English for her sake, even though Maria and Mrs Noriega slipped into Spanish sometimes. Eduardo had no difficulty, but he didn't contribute much to the conversation, just the usual kind of generalities.

The meal was delicious and filling. Maria explained they were eating buenos beans, ribs and sausage. Eduardo leaned back in satisfaction and linked his arms above his head. His shirt stretched across his muscled chest, and the flatness of his stomach showed for a moment. He stood up. 'I'll sort out this week's deliveries before I go, but I'm going down to the village later, to see Luis.'

Sophia Noriega nodded. 'I've done the ground work; you just need to check the figures are correct. Everything is on the desk in the study.'

Claire stood up. 'I'm off to my cottage. Thank you, Maria, the meal was superb. Do you need any help with the washing up?'

Maria, beaming at her appreciation, shook her head.

Mrs Noriega said, 'There's no reason for you to rush off, Claire. You're welcome to stay.'

'That's kind, but I'm tired. It's probably all the fresh air and Maria's excellent cooking. Maria has already filled the fridge for me with breakfast fare, so I'll wish you all a good night and see you tomorrow.' She shoved her chair neatly back under the table and smiled before she left.

Eduardo watched her shadow crossing the yard before he turned away and headed for the study.

Mrs Noriega and Maria chatted as they cleared the table and filled the dishwasher. It had taken a lot of tactical persuasion before Maria accepted the machine; she still pounced gleefully on anything that fell below standards when it was unpacked, and rewashed it. It helped to confirm her belief that washing-up by hand was always more effective.

The two older women were now looking forward to a programme on the TV. Maria picked up her knitting on the way to the sitting room. Claire found out later that no one was sure what she was knitting, and no one ever asked. In the past, she'd snapped people's heads off if they did so.

Even though knitting was now fashionable again, Maria had never let herself be influenced by what was, or was not, fashionable. Maria came from a small village in the hills, but contact these days was intermittent because she had no living relatives.

Claire also heard later from Mrs Noriega that Maria was illegitimate and her mother had never married. It had been a hard time of terrible humiliation for her when she was young, and she'd been eternally grateful that Eduardo's grandmother had taken her in as a housemaid. The Casona de la Esquina was the only real home she'd known.

2

Next morning sunbeams stole between the curtains and fell across Claire's face. She stretched, enjoying the comfort and warmth of the sweet-smelling covers. Looking at her bedside clock, she saw it was quite early and thought briefly about trying to get back to sleep, but knew she was already fired up for the day and ready to go.

She threw back the covers and parted the curtains. Eduardo was already striding across the yard on his way to whatever he was about to do. He looked up, probably attracted by the movement of the curtains, and acknowledged her. She made a rippling wave with her fingers and moved away.

She enjoyed her solitary breakfast and tidied everything away afterwards. She was tidy by nature these days, because her small flat didn't allow much room for her to be messy and her father had been extremely strict about neatness and order.

Claire didn't want to think about her father; he'd ruled them with a fist of iron. Her mother had always tried to balance things out with her love and concern. Picking an apple from the bowl of fruit someone had left on the table, she went across to the barn to study the furniture. She looked forward with pleasure to her first day in Casona de la Esquina.

A couple of hours later, after she'd had plenty of time to examine the waiting furniture and make notes, someone knocked briefly on the door-frame. She looked up and relaxed as Eduardo strolled in, and she started to explain what ought to be done. He followed her around as she pointed out what needed work and attention. His presence heightened her awareness, but she was used to talking to customers and felt business-like enough to explain how she intended to manage things.

Finally, she handed him the calculations she'd worked out for each item. 'I haven't included the wardrobe, but if it's only a damaged foot, that won't be an exorbitant addition.'

He looked at her tally. After a couple of moments when Claire felt the beginnings of trepidation, he said. 'Okay. It seems fair enough. Which item will need the most work, do you think?'

Claire lowered her dark lashes and thought before she looked up; she didn't want to show him how pleased she was. 'The desk. One of the drawers is infected with woodworm. Normally, I'd have to treat every single hole. As you can imagine, that's very time-consuming. As it's part of the back section of the drawer and, as far as I can tell, the problem is confined just to the one patch, I suggest that we replace that section completely. I'll do a replacement that no non-professional would notice.'

He studied her face and said. 'Yes, go ahead. As we have no intention of ever selling the furniture anyway, my main concern is their final appearance and that they are in good shape.'

'It'll look like new when I've finished, I promise! So far, I haven't found any overwhelming problems. I'd like to keep the leather on the desk. It's not damaged and it gives it a special quality. I can replace it, if you wish, but if you'll take my advice I'd leave it alone. It just needs a good clean.'

He ran his hand over its smooth surface. 'Agreed.'

'Good. The desk will take longest to sort out, so I'm going to start on that. When I was training, my boss always said to handle the most complicated task first.'

He nodded. 'I can imagine why. It's the psychological effect of knowing you've conquered the toughest job first.' Hands stuck in his jeans, he asked, 'Didn't you face resentment from the men when you took up this profession? I expect most restorers are men, aren't they?'

Claire answered with quiet assurance. 'Most restorers are still men, but more women are taking it up these days. I didn't let any ill-feeling bother me. I soon found that they stop bickering when you prove you're as good, or even better. Perhaps I shouldn't say so, but women have more patience, and they're often better suited to the kind of detailed and time-consuming work that's involved in this kind of job.'

The corners of his mouth lifted and their eyes locked. He looked down and picked up the sheet of paper bearing Claire's costing notes. 'I'll keep this, if I may, and take a closer look later on.'

'Of course. Some things might even turn out to be cheaper than I've estimated. If that's the case, obviously I'll adjust the final amount. I can type you up a proper estimate if you want one, and naturally I'll keep you informed of progress.'

'As long as you stick to this rough estimate, plus the wardrobe of course, then there's no need. You can check the wardrobe any time. Ask Maria to show it to you.'

He seemed satisfied and Claire was relieved. 'I will, but I've plenty to do at present and I'll come back to that later.'

She paused and looked through the open doors. 'What sort of farm is this? I saw cattle when I arrived. Or were they cows?'

There was teasing in his expression. 'They're beef cattle. We also make hay to feed the cattle in winter, we have fields of corn, potatoes, some sheep, a bit of forestry here and there, and I breed horses.'

'Gosh, that's lots of different things.'

'A disease can wipe out a potato crop overnight, and the same goes for corn or other kinds of crops. The sheep more or less take care of themselves, but they pick up foot rot, worms and such. The forestry work has to be balanced — not cutting down too much too soon, and re-planting so that you have wood for sale in future times. If you vary your sources of income, you have a better chance of surviving in a crisis.'

'And you manage it all on your own?'

He shook his head. 'I couldn't. Pablo is a full-time worker and his wife helps in the house with cleaning. During harvesting time, local helpers fill the gaps. Back in my grandfather's day,' he went on, 'there was a lot more land, and many more workers. The Civil War changed many things. He didn't live to see the farm recover properly. He was against Franco and went off to fight and although he came back, the family had to sell off land to survive. My grandfather was always under pressure from local people who were on the other side of the fence, right up until the restoration of the monarchy.'

'Hmm . . . growing up in a country that takes freedom and democracy for granted, like me, it's hard to understand how people allowed Franco to hang on to power for so long.'

'You just need someone who grabs power and holds on to it in an undemocratic way.' He looked at his watch. 'I'm going to get something to eat. Coming?'

She shook her head. 'I'll have an apple and wait until this evening's meal. If I eat three times a day, I'll look like a barrel.'

He gave her a lengthy look. 'I can't imagine that is ever likely to happen. You're already too thin.'

'I am not! I'm just watching that I don't get fat.'

'Girls like walking skeletons send shivers down my spine.' He turned away and headed towards the kitchen and Maria.

Claire mused that if thin girls sent shivers down his spine, Eduardo Noriega was having a very similar kind of effect on her — but for very different reasons.

* * *

Claire began on the desk. The legs had a desirable patina and apart from cleaning them, she intended to leave them alone. She removed the drawers, burned the damaged pieces, and after protecting the leather with newspaper and masking tape she began to strip and neutralise all the rest. She was still busy when she heard the children's voices; it was nearly three o'clock and they were back from school.

Alisa found her soon afterwards. 'Hello. Can I come in? Uncle Eduardo said we're not to bother you.'

Claire smiled. 'Yes, of course, as long as you promise not to touch anything without my permission.'

Alisa nodded and made herself comfortable nearby.

'Where's Antonio?' Claire asked her.

'Playing Nintendo in his room.'

'What was school like?' Claire went on with her sanding with one hand, dusting frequently in between with a damp cloth in her other hand.

'It was okay. I wish we were near the village, then I could meet someone after school.' Claire nodded sympathetically. 'I like reading, but not all the time

— and Antonio always wants to play such stupid games.'

Claire sympathised. 'My brother was the same. I was always the Indian, the gangster, or the goalkeeper. I was often bored while he was having a wonderful time.'

Alisa nodded. 'We can ride whenever we like, of course. Antonio is a first-class rider, and he enjoys it very much.'

'And you don't?'

'I try not to show it, but I'm a bit frightened because the horses are so big, especially Uncle Eduardo's horses. I fell off one a long time ago when I started, and horses can tell if you're frightened. They seize control, and then things get worse.'

Claire thought how sensible and sensitive Alisa was.

'But don't tell anyone I'm scared, or Antonio will tease me constantly. Can you ride horses?'

'No, I never had the chance. Where I grew up there was no riding school. I expect people's hobbies often depend upon where they grow up and what possibilities there are. I had to go swimming every week, and I didn't like that much, either. My father insisted I went and I hated it.'

Alisa leaned forward and twisted a strand of her hair nervously. 'It's not nice to be frightened, is it?' She swung her gangly legs back and forth beneath her chair.

'No, it isn't. If you don't like riding, why don't you tell your mother? I'm sure she wouldn't want to force you to do something you don't like.'

'Everyone in the family loves riding, so I don't think they'd understand. It's easier just to join in if I can't get out of it.'

'You're not frightened to tell your Uncle Eduardo, are you?'

The little girl shook her head. 'Not really. I just don't want to look silly.'

'You are not being silly. Tell your uncle; I'm sure he'll help. You mustn't be afraid of telling someone.'

'You were afraid and didn't get out of swimming, but I will tell Uncle Eduardo — I promise.' She jumped to her feet. 'I'm going to see Pablo, he said he'd let me feed the chickens.'

'You do that.' The little girl's words struck a chord with Claire. She was right. She hadn't wanted to upset her mother, so she'd kept quiet although she loathed her weekly swimming session with its impossible targets of swimming faster and further and taking part in competitions.

'I'll see you later.'

'I'll be here.' Claire felt sorry for the little girl. It was a pity they were so far away from the village. But she couldn't do much about it. She was here to work. She'd suggest going for a walk with her, or perhaps a game of table tennis later on; that might cheer her up.

* * *

A little while later, on her way back to the barn from the toilet, she heard some male voices and saw Eduardo talking to a middle-aged man in the courtyard. Eduardo gestured her across. Hesitating for a moment, Claire went. There was something about Eduardo that made her feel completely aware of him, and his surroundings. She concentrated on the man at his side.

'Claire this is our neighbour, Philip De Silva.'

Claire smiled at the older man. His face was thin with a domed forehead and bushy brows. He was a lot shorter than Eduardo; his eyes were dark grey and his mouth was formed into a smile. He held out his hand and Eduardo said something to him in Spanish. Claire took his firm grip and guessed he was the father of Juan, the man she'd met on horseback the other day. She felt no aversion and smiled back. He rattled away again and Eduardo translated.

'He says he remembers my grandmother, and you are the first English woman he's met since then. He wants to know if all of you are so pretty.'

Claire chuckled. 'Thank him for the compliment, please, but I'm nothing special.'

Eduardo tilted his head to the side. 'I agree with him. You are pretty.'

Claire felt embarrassed and tongue-tied and was glad when Maria interrupted their conversation. She came towards them carrying a loaf of bread, and another packet that probably contained cake. Philip De Silva put his arm round Maria's shoulder, hugged her and accepted her gifts. There was a loud exchange of words in Spanish, and laughter. Even though she didn't understand, Claire could tell they all liked one another.

Philip tucked the offerings under one arm and picked up something he'd come to borrow from Eduardo with the other. Unable to do more than lift his loaded hands in farewell, he smiled at them and set off across the fields again.

Maria and Eduardo watched him go. Maria said. 'Such a shame. He deserves a better life. If only Juan and Elena did their bit, they'd make things better all round.'

Eduardo nodded silently.

* * *

By the time Claire had showered and changed, and gone across for the evening meal, the children were already in bed.

Claire wondered if Eduardo had a girlfriend. Most likely he did, she thought; he was young and single. She contented herself with eyeing him across the table and reflecting that he was definitely a man worth knowing. He worked hard physically and he carried the responsibility for his mother, Maria, and Pablo's family.

She lingered a little longer this evening over a glass of wine before Eduardo eventually excused himself with a pre-arranged meeting with someone in the village. Claire chatted to the two older women for a while, and they asked her about her family and her work.

When she got back to her cottage, she was quite content to settle down in a corner with a paperback. She was satisfied with today's progress on the desk and she was looking forward to tomorrow.

* * *

Claire's heightened awareness of her surroundings grew with every passing day. Perhaps it was because the farmstead was off the main road with fields all around in every direction. It was a quiet, solitary atmosphere, very peaceful.

Which also meant that the work was going well. She estimated that the various polishing processes would take at least four days, plus time for the finish to harden completely.

Once she began polishing, the desk gained a lovely rich colour. She already planned to use the time between the bouts of polishing to replace the damaged woodworm section in the back of the drawer. When that was finished, she'd then only need to touch up the scratches on the leather finish, give it an application of leather cream, and ensure that the drawers glided smoothly.

Claire was busy on one of the stages of polishing when she heard the sound of horses' hooves clattering on the stone surface in the yard. She was used to seeing Eduardo riding out to distant parts of the farmstead to work and, at first, she'd stopped furtively to admire his horsemanship, and follow his progress. Now, a few days later, she didn't do so any more because it was a silly distraction.

She didn't want to think fanciful thoughts about Eduardo Noriega. She'd be on her way home again in a couple of weeks' time. She concentrated on stroking the polish into wood in the correct way, and was almost startled when she heard voices laughing and then footsteps coming towards the barn. Eduardo knocked on the door-frame. He came in with a tall slim woman, and was followed by Juan De Silva.

'Good morning. This is Elena De Silva, and her brother, Juan. They're our neighbours. You met their father the other day.'

Juan met her eyes boldly. 'You don't need to introduce us, Eduardo. I've already met Claire; the other day, near your grandmother's cottage.'

Eduardo's brows lifted and, under his scrutiny, Claire needed a moment to adjust. She wasn't answerable to Eduardo, but she didn't want to displease him. She hurried to explain. 'I went with the children to the pond and Juan was out riding.'

'Oh, I see. Philip told them what you are doing here, and they wanted to see for themselves. I hope you don't mind?'

Claire was still holding a polishing pad. 'No, of course not.'

She looked at the young woman by his side. Elena had a shapely figure and a narrow waist, and her riding outfit showed off her slim hips to perfection. Her pristine white blouse was tucked into riding jodhpurs and shiny black boots completed the picture. Her face was classical in shape and her colouring was very attractive, with dark hair, a tanned complexion and dark grey eyes like her father.

She slapped her riding whip against one of her gloved hands and gave Claire a smile that didn't quite reach her eyes. Claire guessed that Miss De Silva was more interested in finding out what Claire Coleman was like than about Claire's work.

Elena circled the desk as she reluctantly admitted, 'Yes, I see what you mean, Eduardo. It looks like a completely different piece of furniture now. Who would have thought it could look so good?' She smiled acidly.

Claire didn't know if she should comment or not. In the end, she remained silent and waited. Eduardo was at Elena's shoulder, and the woman glanced up at him in an affectionate way and continued, 'Surprising what can be achieved, isn't it?'

Eduardo gave Elena a smile and for a moment, Claire felt resentful. Elena reached out towards the desk with one of her gloved hands and Claire hurried to say, 'Don't touch! Please. The polish is still very fresh. It has to be really hard before anyone can touch it.'

Elena flushed and looked a little irritated.

Juan laughed. 'That's what I like; a woman with spirit.'

Colouring slightly, Claire rushed to add, 'No offence intended, but if I have to re-strip and re-polish, then I'm afraid it'll cost Eduardo more money.'

Elena nodded and managed to hide her irritation. She'd seen enough, and turned to Eduardo. 'We came near lunchtime because I'm hoping that we can share yours. I haven't seen you or your mother for ages.'

Eduardo had been viewing the desk with interest while listening to the conversation.

'You're very welcome, you know that. Maria always has something bubbling on the stove.'

Elena's laugh tinkled. 'That's good. Let's go over, before you find something more urgent to do and disappear again.'

'I had planned to get on with repairing some fencing, but I may as well stop for lunch now. What about you, Claire? Won't you join us — make an exception for once?'

Juan leaned against the doorpost and drawled, 'Yes, do join us, Claire. It will be much more fun with you around.'

Eduardo looked at him as if he was irritated for a second and Elena's brows furrowed briefly too. Claire wondered if Elena was peeved because she thought that employers and employees shouldn't mix, or because she wanted Eduardo's sole attention.

Claire didn't want to be a participant; she shook her head. 'Thanks, but I want to finish off this layer of polish. I have some fruit and a flask of tea; that's all I need.'

Elena rounded the table, and clenching her riding whip in her fist, she swept out of the barn with a curt, 'Goodbye, then.'

She expected Eduardo to follow and he did, but not before Juan exited ahead of him. Juan looked back at Claire, and shrugged with mock resignation before he left. Eduardo followed him and muttered with a touch of defiance in his voice, 'See you this evening, then.'

Claire followed their progress as they walked towards the main house. She heard their voices echoing across the yard until they reached the far side of the farmhouse.

Claire didn't understand why the visit bothered her. Were Eduardo and Elena more than just friends? If so, Elena had no reason to show resentment or jealousy.

Claire smiled to herself when she considered her present appearance; it was enough to send any man running. She never bothered with make-up when she was working and her hair was tied back out of the way in an old cotton scarf. She was wearing a shapeless stained overall and rubber gloves. Even her shoes were covered in polish, paints and blobs of dried glue.

She was no competition for the beautiful, well turned-out Elena De Silva — or a temptation for the handsome Juan.

Juan was clearly used to flaunting his attractions in front of the opposite sex and she supposed that perhaps some girls enjoyed that sort of thing.

She didn't. You simply couldn't trust any man who liked to flirt in such an outrageous manner, she felt. Claire polished harder. She wasn't really surprised, later at dinner, to hear that Eduardo had gone out with friends that evening.

3

Next day, Claire was busy measuring and sanding a piece of wood for the drawer. Alisa's voice interrupted her as the child dashed into the barn; she was excited and her cheeks were red. 'Claire, we're going on an outing with Uncle Eduardo to the beach tomorrow.'

Claire picked up a plane and began to remove a couple of thin layers from the piece of the replacement wood. She looked up. 'Are you? That's good. I expect you'll enjoy yourself a lot. I love the seaside, too.'

Alisa nodded. 'Will you come with us?'

She looked up at the little girl's animated expression. 'It's nice of you to think of asking me, Alisa, but it's a family outing. You can tell me all about it afterwards.'

A dark, tall figure filled the open

doorway. 'If you'd like to come, we'll be pleased to have you along. I promised Alisa and Antonio we'd go last weekend, but I had to call it off at the last minute. I thought it might be a chance for you to see some of the coastline. We have some really lovely beaches and coves.'

Confused by the sudden invitation, Claire's throat was dry and colour rushed to her face when she met his eyes. 'Actually, I was hoping I could finish the drawer off tomorrow.'

He made a clicking sound with his tongue and shook his head. 'Maria will skin you alive if you work on a Sunday.'

'Oh! I'd forgotten that it's Sunday; is it that important?'

'Maria is a strict Catholic and hasn't missed mass on Sunday as long as I can remember. According to Maria, no one should work on Sunday. Be warned — I have the devil's own job to persuade her that I have to sometimes if an emergency crops up on Sunday with one of the animals.'

'But she doesn't object to family outings?'

'No, because it's not work. Would you like to come, or would you prefer to curl up with a good book in the bath like my sister used to do?'

Alisa joined in. 'Do come, Claire. It will be fun.'

Claire smiled. 'Who can resist? All right, I'll come.'

Alisa clapped her hands and Eduardo smiled.

'I thought we could leave after breakfast and make a day of it. The children have to be back to go to bed early because of school next day — ' Alisa groaned — 'but that still gives us plenty of time. Maria usually gives us a picnic. She's probably glad to get rid of us for a few hours. I know my mother is visiting a friend of hers tomorrow afternoon, so Maria will be free to go to church and then sit back and knit to her heart's content.'

His smile had a silly effect on her and she couldn't help but feel slightly exhilarated by the idea of spending the day with him and the children. 'Right. I'll be ready whenever you are, then.'

Alisa shouted, 'Hurrah!' and Eduardo lifted his hand in a wave before he turned and disappeared.

Alisa was clearly satisfied. Claire hoped Antonio liked the idea, too. She had a feeling she'd broken through his initial reticence, so it should be fun. She felt extra pleasure as she went on working until late that day.

When everyone gathered later for the evening meal, the children joined them because it was the weekend, so there was a lot more noise, jollity and excitement. Mrs Noriega tried to curb their high spirits but Alisa prattled continuously about the arranged day trip tomorrow, even infecting Antonio with her enthusiasm.

Eduardo eyed Claire across the table and shrugged his shoulders before he turned his attention to the children. 'There'll be no running off on your own, no climbing up crumbling rock faces, and no back-answers when you are told to do something, okay? If you play up, I won't take you again and I'll tell your mother that you are badly brought up.'

The children knew it wasn't too serious and he was teasing them. Antonio asked, 'What about Claire? Does she have to do as she is told?'

Tongue in cheek, Eduardo returned, 'But of course, because I'm the boss.'

Antonio studied Claire. 'I think she's likely to cause more trouble than we do, she's not used to being bossed around. She's her own boss.'

Eduardo laughed and looked at Claire. 'I think you may be right, but I'm willing to take the chance.'

* * *

Claire had a leisurely breakfast. She didn't have a swimming costume — she hadn't reckoned with summer outings to the beach — but she did have shorts and a T-shirt, and that's what she decided to wear. Her legs were pale, but shapely and long. She took more time than usual to get ready and avoided asking herself why she was bothering. Alisa and Antonio wouldn't care if she had horns on her head!

When she heard the children, she picked up her backpack and walked across the yard to the farmhouse, where they were waiting excitedly near Eduardo's car. She walked towards them. Alisa was skipping around in circles. 'Uncle Eduardo is getting the picnic from Maria.'

Antonio's head was hidden; he was loading some stuff into the boot of the car, but he looked up and grinned at her when he heard her voice.

Eduardo joined them with a bulky basket. 'Morning, Claire. I think Maria has given us enough to last a whole week.' He smiled at her and her pulse rate increased.

She returned his smile. 'Morning. She probably can't bear the idea of anyone going hungry, can she?'

He put the basket into the boot, and indicated towards the car's interior with a wave. 'That's true. So, we're ready — let's go.' He looked at Antonio and Alisa. 'You two . . . in the back!'

Claire got into the passenger seat and fastened the belt.

By the time they reached the main road, Antonio was already clicking away on his Nintendo. Alisa smiled at her via the rear mirror and Claire felt a surge of affection for the little girl. She had such a sunny disposition.

Claire looked out of the window and listened as Eduardo and Alisa pointed out things along the route.

There was soft music on the radio and Claire concentrated on enjoying the journey; it gave her a chance to see some more of the local countryside. Eduardo glanced at her sometimes and Claire reminded herself that she hadn't come here to start fantasising about a man she hadn't known existed until a few weeks ago; someone who might even be Elena De Silva's boyfriend. He was her employer, an interesting man, but that's as far as her interest should ever go.

They reached the coast in a little over an hour. Eduardo had chosen a beach that he knew; a particularly beautiful one that curved in a lazy arc and had soft golden sand.

Antonio put his Nintendo away promptly when he realised they'd arrived. He and Alisa couldn't wait to get out of the car and hurtle down the series of steps that had been cut into the rocks. Eduardo gave the children some playthings to carry, while he and Claire shared the remaining rugs, picnic basket, flasks and their own backpacks.

The day wasn't hot, but it was warm and the sun was shining. Claire thought it was perfect. In mid-summer, the beach would be packed with tourists, but today the sands were only spotted with visitors and temperatures were enjoyable.

Eduardo suggested that they spread the rugs near the grass-covered incline below the rock face. It was far away from the sea, but sheltered from the wind. The children wanted to tear off towards the ocean right away but Eduardo insisted they waited until someone could go with them. They had to be content scrabbling about in nearby rock pools, looking for crabs.

Watching them, Eduardo said, 'It's too risky to leave them on their own. We're too far away and even if we can see them, by the time I got there it might be too late.'

Claire nodded. 'We can take it in turns to go with them. I expect they'll be quite happy to play around here, near us, once the first excitement of going for a swim has worn off.'

Eduardo was divesting himself of his chinos and polo shirt. He was wearing swim shorts in bright Hawaiian colours. He looked good; his long legs were brown and firm, and his lean body was wide-shouldered. The sea breezes played with his hair and he pushed it impatiently out of the way.

He called across to the two children. 'Hey, you two — ready?'

Antonio and Alisa didn't need a second invitation.

He looked at Claire. 'Are you coming? If you have anything valuable you can lock it in the boot of the car.'

Claire shook her head. 'I don't have a swimsuit with me. I'll stay here and guard everything. Enjoy yourselves.'

Eduardo removed his watch and handed it to her with a smile before he ran after the children who were already on the move. His long strides soon caught up with them and Claire heard the children squealing as a race ensued to see who'd reach the water first.

They were gone a while, and Claire watched their diminutive figures having fun. At first, she was grateful for the warmth of her cardigan as she sat on the rug with her arms wrapped around her knees, but by the time she saw Eduardo and the children coming back, it was warm enough to discard it again.

Flopping down beside her, Eduardo

grabbed a towel and began to dry himself. Seawater was trickling down his face and Claire longed to reach out and touch him. She didn't, of course, and busied herself instead in helping the children into their towel robes. Immediately comforted by the warmth, they wanted something to eat and Claire proceeded to search the plastic containers and found them some sandwiches. She laughed. 'We've only just arrived and you're already two hungry bears.'

A voice at her side said, 'Make that three hungry bears! Can I have one too?'

Claire obliged, laughing softly as she handed him a sandwich.

Their hunger stilled for a moment, Alisa and Antonio picked up their buckets and spades and set to work creating a sandcastle. It began with a small inner castle with strong defences, then the inner walls were extended, towers were added, outer walls were created and finally a moat and a drawbridge materialised.

Claire and Eduardo watched with interest, but relaxed. They made back-rests of sand and began to read. The wind was warm but blustery and it plastered Claire's T-shirt to her body and messed her hair, but she enjoyed the salty air and the feeling of warm sand under her bare feet.

Up above, seabirds calling noisily to each other circled in the blue heaven. Most of all, she enjoyed being with Eduardo and the children, and from the smiling glances he gave her, he was enjoying himself too. When both of them happened to put their books aside for a moment, he asked, 'What do you think? It's a nice beach, isn't it?'

'Yes — it's lovely.'

'Would you like to swim? I'm sure there is somewhere nearby where you could buy a costume.'

Claire shoved her wind-tossed curls out of her face. 'I'm not mad about swimming any more. I'm fine, thanks.'

'What does that mean? You were, but

you're not any more? Or you never were?'

Staring straight ahead, she answered, 'My father more or less forced me to join our local swimming club when I was a child. In the beginning, the other kids teased me when the trainer wasn't looking because I wasn't very good. Once I could cope, it didn't matter quite so much and I made friends but I still hated it. He insisted I went, no matter what.'

He viewed the two children, struggling to widen the moat even more. He was silent for a moment. 'Why didn't your mother put a stop to it?'

'She didn't know how much I disliked it. She still doesn't.'

'Why didn't you tell her?'

Her forced laugh had a sharp edge to it. 'Because my father was a bully and ruled the house like a tyrant. What he said was law. He would only have had another of his tirades about the right way to bring up children — his way.'

Eduardo looked across sharply and

Claire went on, 'He was in the regular army for fifteen years. When he came out, he was a sales representative. I think he disliked his job, but he never talked about it. He probably missed the regulation of military life and tried to create his own little territorial army in our house.

'My mother is a love, but she wasn't capable of standing up to him, and it only got worse as we grew older, although my brother didn't seem to mind as much. Perhaps he liked being forced to play football and keeping his room tidy. I don't like being forced to do anything. Moreover, I guessed that Father didn't think much of girls. If I'd been a boy, he would have liked me more.'

'Surely not?'

Claire gave a dry laugh. 'That's my theory, anyway. When my brother went to university Dad got more touchy and irritable, and one day he gave Mum a black eye when they were arguing about something she'd bought without asking him first. It probably was accidental, but it proved too much even for her.'

Claire shrugged sadly then went on, 'Gary was at university, I was in training, so she packed up and we went to live with my gran. It was wonderful to be free of his control. Mum found herself a job in a flower shop and got a divorce. She owns the shop now and employs someone to help her. I think he tried to talk her round, but by then she could see how he'd controlled her life, and ours. She didn't love him any more.'

'And . . . do you ever see him now?'

'No, and it won't bother me if I never see him again. Perhaps that sounds bad, but he spoiled all the fun. You can't go back and re-live your childhood. He wasn't physically cruel to me, but there's more than one way to be cruel to children. I don't know if he realises what he did wrong and quite honestly, I don't care. He eventually remarried, and is probably bossing someone else around now.'

Eduardo reached across, and before she realised it, he had trapped her hand between his, his expression full of sympathy. 'Don't let it affect the way you think or act forever, Claire. You've come through it undamaged. You're self-supporting, you do interesting work, and you're independent.' His gaze was direct and very disconcerting.

Colour flamed on her face but she met his glance. Her heart was pounding and she hoped he couldn't tell.

Awkwardly she withdrew her hand and smoothed her hair out of her eyes, then gave him a shaky smile. 'It's made me more sensitive about bossy, domineering men, I suppose, but I'm not a man-hater if that's what you mean. I'm just more cautious. Perhaps if my father had stayed in the army and in the kind of environment where he felt happiest, he would have spent less time training us at home.'

She distractedly brushed some sand from her feet. 'What was your father like?'

'Great,' Eduardo replied gently. 'He was very understanding, very supportive. He died suddenly six years ago. He worried too much about the farm and about family tradition. The family owned more land and were wealthy in earlier times and I suspect he thought he must find a way to reclaim past glories. My grandfather must have lost a packet of money in his time, and my father spent all his married life trying to increase our income and capital. He wanted to regain the influence the family had had in the past. He married into the family, and I think that made him more determined to make good. He probably worried himself to death.'

'And you? You don't worry about the farm?'

They were interrupted by Antonio and Alisa for a moment. They came with buckets and asked if they could go for seawater.

Eduardo nodded towards the nearby rock pools. 'You can get plenty of water there. No need to run back and forth to the sea.'

They were happy with the suggestion and ran off.

He gave his attention to Claire again. As he turned to look at her, she saw there was sand on his arm and wished she was brave enough to brush it away.

'Yes, of course I worry,' he told her. 'Anyone who runs a farm worries continually, but my father's death was a lesson. I know that I can't make miracles happen, I just do the best I can. I've diversified our sources of income and I'm always looking for others. Some years are good and some are bad. Thank goodness, things are improving at the moment. We don't owe the bank any money any more, so I can invest in new machinery. I'd like more capital to cover emergencies, but I don't lose any sleep over it. All farmers face problems and complications; farming has always been hard work, risky and completely dependent on nature; no one can control nature.'

She nodded. 'Yet you still thought it was important to have your gran's furniture restored? Perhaps you ought to have kept the money for emergencies instead.'

His smile was wide, his teeth strikingly white against his tanned face, and her heart hammered foolishly.

'Perhaps.' He looked thoughtfully out to sea. 'I owed it to Gran; I promised her and I always keep my promises. We can afford it at the moment.' He turned his attention to her face again. 'Or do you want to do yourself out of a job?'

She laughed, and his eyes twinkled when she replied, 'No, of course not — you're helping my business to survive!'

'I'll show you Gran's cottage one day,' he said. 'It's in the middle of a field not far from the house. It's dilapidated and needs doing up. It needs a generator for a start, but I don't know if it's worth bothering because it's so isolated. It was Gran's special retreat. We loved going there when we were kids. She made us high tea, and we loved the tiny cucumber sandwiches and fairy cakes and all the rest . . . ' He suddenly pulled himself back to the present. 'Talking of food, what about the picnic? I expect the kids are growing hungry again.'

Claire was glad to have something else to think about. They unpacked the lunch and arranged it on the rugs.

Suddenly and quite unexpectedly, Eduardo leaned forward and kissed her softly, his mouth warm and salty on hers. 'Don't think about the past, Claire,' he murmured. 'The present is all that's important.'

He got up and brushed his hands free of sand. 'I'll tell them to come. I don't suppose they would of their own free will, even if they are hungry.'

Even though Claire didn't want to focus on him, his kiss had shattered that resolve. Her lips were tingling from his kiss and her body longed for more. Was he just flirting? Claire couldn't believe he was that kind of man . . . so perhaps he and Elena weren't a twosome after all? She touched her lips with the tips of her fingers, reliving the moment.

She didn't feel awkward talking to him about her father. She'd never spoken to anyone about her childhood, and she wondered why she could do so with such ease with Eduardo Noriega.

He climbed the rocks and gestured to the children to come; they'd wandered further away. It took a bit of persuasion, but eventually they came. She watched them all returning with the sun on their backs.

She busied herself with plastic cups and food containers. Even if he were free, their lives were poles apart and it would never work.

They shared a filling lunch as the sun shone down. Claire relaxed and began to enjoy herself again.

After lunch, they helped the children stabilise the castle walls, played a game of crazy football and then threw a Frisbee around for a while. Eduardo looked as if he was enjoying himself almost as much as Alisa and Antonio. The children were determined to go for a swim again so Eduardo shrugged, smiled at Claire, and obliged them.

When they returned, they dried off and everyone agreed to go for a stroll along the beach. They walked to the end of the long sands as far as the next bend in the coastline, the children racing ahead and gathering shells on the way.

The sea was a deep, clear green and the cliffs jutted sharply out into the seawater. When they reached the point where the rocks cut off any further progress, the children stood waiting.

Claire climbed one of the rocks, stopping to push some wind-whipped hair out of her face and watch the waves dashing against the speckled boulders in her path. Eduardo joined her and when they turned to go back, he reached up to help her down. He held her hand for longer than necessary and she tingled at his touch. They looked at each other silently for a second or so before the children brought them back to earth.

'Can we have some ice cream?'

Eduardo groaned theatrically. 'Only if you get dressed properly — and then there's no more swimming today. We're not going for ices and then back to the beach.'

'Then we want to go for a swim now and then for an ice cream after!'

Eduardo laughed. 'Okay.'

* * *

Later, when the children were dressed again, they packed everything up and took it back to the car. They strolled down a wide promenade bordering the cliff, edged with trees and flowering shrubs, towards the cafés. They were busy, but they soon found a comfortable corner overlooking the cliffs. The children took a long time deciding what to choose, but Eduardo and Claire were indulgent and waited.

By the time they'd slowly ambled

back to his car, the sun had lost most of its power and the air was cooling. Looking at his watch, Eduardo declared it was time to go home. The children groaned and wanted to go down to the beach once more, but Eduardo was firm.

'You have school tomorrow. It's time to go.'

As soon as they were on the road once more, Alisa's head fell to the side and she slept while Antonio stared listlessly out of the window and ignored his Nintendo. Once back at the farm, Alisa woke up yawning. The children would sleep well tonight. They said their goodbyes to Claire and helped to carry things back into the house.

Claire picked up her backpack and turned to Eduardo. Her heart hammered against her ribs. 'Thanks for a really lovely day. I enjoyed it. I think the children had a great time, didn't they?'

He nodded. They shared a moment of mutual awareness and then he said, 'I hope we'll so something similar again before you leave, Claire . . . '

The sound of an approaching car cut the moment short. The wheels of a bottle-green sports car squealed to a stop and Juan got out.

He acknowledged Eduardo briefly, then immediately took Claire's hand and gave it an old-fashioned kiss. 'I've come to invite my English rose out for a meal. I will take you somewhere special.' He eyed her shorts and T-shirt and his glance tarried appreciatively on her long legs. 'I'll give you ten minutes to change into something suitable.'

Claire didn't need to fabricate an excuse. She replied truthfully, 'Thanks, Juan, but we've been out with the children at the beach all day and I'm too tired to even contemplate going anywhere else, I'm afraid.'

Vaguely she was conscious of Eduardo's tall figure in the background and something that looked like a scowl on his face.

'Oh, come on. A few hours in a posh restaurant, soft music, good wine and some dancing. You can't turn that down.' Juan's dark eyes sparkled, and Claire wished she could feel more comfortable about him. She withdrew her hand and ran it over her own hair.

'No, honestly — thanks for inviting me. Anyway, I have nothing with me to wear that would be even halfway suitable.'

She could tell he didn't like the rebuff. He flicked a sharp look in her direction. It was only momentary, but Juan De Silva clearly didn't like to be turned down. He glared at her, frowning. 'You're sure?'

Claire tried to give him a consoling smile. 'Quite sure, but thanks anyway — another time, perhaps.'

Juan considered her for a moment and then shrugged. 'I'll have to find someone else for tonight then; I've booked a table.'

She looked pointedly at her watch. 'I'll leave you to it, then. I'm dying for a cup of tea.'

Juan recovered enough to chuckle.

'How English can anyone get?' he said.

Turning away, Claire replied, 'I suppose I'm as English as anyone born in England can be. See you later, Eduardo. Bye, Juan.' She was glad to escape.

Juan saluted Eduardo and climbed into his car. Turning too fast, he tooted the horn and threw up dust as he sped towards the main road.

On her way back to the cottage, she called to check on the drying progress of the desk, glad that she could disappear to her cottage and be on her own once more.

After the evening meal, she would hole up with her book and try not to spend the evening wondering if Eduardo regretted kissing her.

Unknown to her, Eduardo had studied her departing figure intently before he turned away. The expression in his eyes was indecipherable; his back was ramrod straight as he hurried indoors.

4

The following morning, Claire decided her next piece of work would be the chest of drawers. Crawling on all fours, she looked underneath. Some of the supporting blocks on the underside needed replacing because they'd been lost through age and damp conditions. To anyone who didn't know better, they looked like unimportant details, but Claire knew how they contributed to the solidity of a piece of furniture.

One of the bracket feet needed to be replaced, the base of one of the drawers was rotten, some of the runners were worn, and she'd need to make a new back-plate for two of the drawers — one was missing and the other was damaged. She'd also need to replace a pivot hinge, and then came the inevitable job of cleaning and re-polishing. She went to look for someone to help her move the chest from the wall to the centre of the room. She found Pablo, busy loading sacks onto a tractor's trailer. With lots of gesturing, she managed to make him understand she needed his help and he followed her into the barn.

Claire pointed to the chest of drawers and then to where she needed it. He understood and mentioned Eduardo's name. She guessed he meant they should wait for Eduardo. She shook her head; removing the drawers, she bent down on one side and waited for him to join her on the other. He took off his peaked hat and rubbed his hand across his face. Deciding that she was clearly a determined woman, he gave in, replaced the cap and walked over.

It was heavy, but Claire had helped transport heavy pieces before. Her master carpenter had always told her how important it was to lift something in the correct way and Claire had never forgotten. She knew that she wouldn't have attempted it if she felt she couldn't cope. It was heavy, but she managed. Pablo grinned when it was in place. They tipped it on its back so that she could work on the underside easily.

He patted her on the shoulder before he left and Claire called 'Gracias!' after him several times, before he disappeared, muttering to himself — no doubt about the strange habits of foreign women.

She needed six or seven new blocks to replace the missing or damaged ones along the skirt of the chest. She measured the old ones and began to saw appropriate pieces to shape and sand them. Horses' hooves echoed on the yard outside and footsteps came in her direction.

A satisfying feeling of pleasure spread through her insides; she expected Eduardo. Her anticipation was dampened when she saw Juan De Silva standing in the doorway instead. He cut out most of the light, and Claire felt uncomfortable. She didn't like his sharply assessing eyes as they travelled over her old jeans and washed-out T-shirt.

'Ah, our working girl; busy again, I see.'

Forcing herself to be polite, she said, 'Morning, Juan. If you want to see Eduardo, he's out somewhere. Pablo can tell you where he is.'

There was an edge to his voice. 'I didn't come to see Eduardo.' His voice softened slightly. 'I came to see you.'

'Really.' Unconsciously, Claire wetted her lips because she felt uncomfortable with this man. 'Why?'

He followed the movement of her tongue with interest. He took a step forward and Claire stiffened. She had to force herself not to step back; she didn't like men who were over-assertive.

'You didn't want to come out with me last night. I decided to ask you to come with me today instead — to a riding competition.'

Flustered, Claire felt increasingly steam-rollered. She stared at him with complete surprise on her face and struggled to maintain a friendly tone. 'Thanks for the offer — it's well meant, I'm sure, but I came here to work, so I really don't have much leisure time.'

His lips twisted into a cynical smile. He clearly expected it would be a foregone conclusion that she'd accept; he was one of those men who assumed he'd always get what he wanted.

'You don't have to work twenty-four hours a day, do you?'

She managed a tremulous smile and hoped that she didn't look as nervous as she felt. 'Look, Juan, this is nothing personal, truly. I work all day, and when I've had my evening meal I'm usually happy to spend the rest of the day peacefully on my own.'

He leaned in close to her with an expression that set her teeth on edge. 'I'm only asking you to sacrifice a couple of hours, or does our hard-working Eduardo keep your nose to the grindstone?'

Claire could feel his breath on her face and she felt harassed. She had no real reason to dislike him, but her instincts told her she wouldn't like his company. He was too sure of himself and he seemed to have too much leisure time for someone who came from a farming background. 'I just want to get the work done as efficiently as possible. I'm here to work on this commission, I'm not here for pleasure.'

He was silent and the tension increased. Claire wondered how she could get rid of him. She didn't like his reproachful eyes. He wasn't used to women refusing his company.

And it seemed that suddenly Eduardo was there. 'Is everything all right, Claire?'

'Yes . . . yes, thanks.' She was always glad to see him, but never more so than at this moment.

Juan gave her a parting glance and without another word, he took off, without even acknowledging Eduardo.

Eduardo stared after him and there was a pause where he looked grim. 'The trouble with Juan is that he's a womaniser — and lazy, too. If he did some work on the family farm it would not only help his father, it would fill in the time he wastes on pointless escapades. It's nothing to do with me, Claire — but please be careful.'

She pulled herself together and looked up. His nearness was playing havoc with her stomach, which was doing little flips as she looked up into his eyes. 'He came here to invite me out again and he seems to think he's irresistible. I probably dented his pride a little when I refused again.' She was silenced by Eduardo's dark expression. Was he was angry with Juan, or with her? It was hard to tell.

She took a deep breath and tried to calm herself. There was still an undercurrent between them; his gaze settled briefly on her mouth and she felt goose bumps forming on her arms. Why did she reject Juan — and why did the mere hope of a kiss from Eduardo make her mind flutter like a trapped butterfly?

He stuck his hands into his jeans pockets and stepped back. 'You're sure you're all right?'

She nodded and ran her hands through her burnished curls, rubbed the surface of her cheeks. 'Yes, I'm fine.'

He nodded. 'I met Pablo and he told me how the two of you moved the chest of drawers. I came to tell you to let us know if you want anything moved in future. There's no necessity for you to lift heavy furniture with two men around to do it for you.'

She gave him a weak smile. 'Thanks.'

Her grey eyes met his dark brown ones and they were each busy with their own silent thoughts until he broke the stillness. 'If you're okay, I'll get back to my work and leave you to yours.'

She nodded. 'I'm fine. See you this evening.'

'Yes, till later.'

He strode out of the shadowy barn into the sunlight beyond, his tall figure soon lost to sight.

Claire tried to concentrate on her

work and to push Juan De Silva out of her mind. She measured, sawed, and sandpapered. After a while she'd very nearly forgotten about Juan De Silva . . . but only because she had finished comparing the two men, and was worrying instead about the effect Eduardo Noriega was having on her.

* * *

She was contented to see that the desk was drying well and she could continue with the next piece, since she aimed to finish the repairs to the drawer by this afternoon.

She was surprised when Maria popped her head round the door and came in, wiping her hands on her apron. Maria wandered unhurriedly around the desk, then sat down on a nearby chair. 'It looks very nice, almost like new. You are good at your job.'

Claire laughed. 'Coming from you, that's praise indeed. You're a great cook and I'm a good restorer. We're both good at our jobs.'

Maria chuckled. 'Yes, I suppose you're right. We both work with our hands, only the results are slightly different.'

Claire reached for her flask. 'Would you like a cup of coffee?'

Maria looked surprised and considered. 'Yes, why not. Do you have some sugar?'

Claire handed her a jar with sugar and a spoon, and a mug of coffee. Maria grasped the mug with age-spotted hands, made herself comfortable and leaned back. 'Did you enjoy yourself at the beach?' she asked.

Claire leaned against a nearby supporting beam and crossed her arms. She could honestly answer, 'Yes, very much. The kids seemed to enjoy it and that was the whole point of going. I benefited from the sea air and enjoyed your tasty picnic, of course.'

'Elena turned up just after you'd left and she wasn't at all happy that she wasn't invited.'

Surprised by the sudden turn in the conversation, Claire looked down, feeling a little embarrassed, and then back at Maria again. 'Really?'

'Everyone thought they'd end up married. I didn't. They're not suited.'

Increasingly confused by the twists and turns in Maria's conversation, Claire asked, 'Eduardo and Elena?'

Maria nodded. 'Elena made a big mistake once, when they were young and Eduardo hasn't forgotten it.'

Claire desperately wanted to know more, but decided not to ask any questions. It might show she was too interested about things that were none of her concern.

But Maria continued to supply the information anyway. 'In those days the farm wasn't doing well. His father had died unexpectedly and Eduardo was left trying to sort out the chaos. He didn't know very much about farming, either — he studied some high-fangled business management at university, you see, and was all geared up to use what he'd learned in the outside world before coming back home.

'Elena has always had her eye on the money and thought she was entitled to something better; I think she has an adding machine instead of a brain!' She laughed bitterly. 'All of a sudden, she figured that Eduardo might not be the good investment she always thought he'd be. They grew up together — neighbouring farms, similar age — everyone expected it would all end up with lace and wedding bells one day . . . '

Claire tried to stem the flow. 'Maria, do you really think you should be telling me all this?'

Maria brushed her qualms aside. 'Why not? Don't tell me that you're not interested in Eduardo yourself?'

Claire coloured and tried to laugh it off. It was clear that Maria obviously didn't hold Elena in much esteem — especially if she'd treated her beloved Eduardo badly.

Maria took a sip of coffee and

continued the story. 'Well, when Elena decided the prospects here weren't so rosy, she went hunting elsewhere. The De Silva family have relations in Madrid and she reckoned that in a cosmopolitan place like that, she'd soon find what she was looking for. I believe she almost landed a banker . . . almost, but not quite.

'We never saw him, but we know he was very rich, very influential and, unfortunately for Elena, he was also clever,' Maria went on. 'He saw right through her, and realised she was out to get him for his money and connections. He played her along for a time until he got bored and found someone else.

'Once he'd dropped her, and there were still no other better prospects in sight, she opted to come back to her father. By then, Eduardo had sorted out the worst of the problems and suddenly she decided he wasn't such a bad prospect after all . . . '

Claire felt uncomfortable listening, but admitted to herself that the opportunity to satisfy her own curiosity about Eduardo was too great, so she remained silent and let Maria continue with her story.

'Eduardo didn't ignore her, he still doesn't — how can he? The De Silvas' farm borders this one — and there were no broken promises or such, but I'm sure that Eduardo learned his lesson. So Elena soon found she couldn't steamroller him any more.

'I'd like to ask him about Elena but he'd bite my head off.' Maria shrugged. 'I think she's playing a waiting game for now, hoping that if she hangs around for long enough, Eduardo will take her for lack of finding anyone better.

'Elena is making the same mistake now that she did in the past; she thinks she understands Eduardo, but she doesn't.'

'I'm not surprised that he's not likely to tell you what he thinks about Elena,' Claire mused. 'Who wants to lay their soul on the line?' She picked up her mug from the working bench and took a sip.

Impatiently Maria answered, 'I've known Eduardo since the day he was born. He doesn't need to tell me anything. Most of the time I can guess what he's thinking.'

With tongue in cheek, Claire smiled and said, 'Then perhaps it would be better for Eduardo and everyone else if he gets married as soon as possible — either to Elena or someone else — if only to put an end to all the speculation!'

'I agree! I keep telling him he should settle down and get himself a family. He just tells me I'm an interfering old woman and I should mind my own business.'

Claire spluttered and laughed awkwardly. 'That's direct of him but, if you don't mind me saying so, I think he's old enough to sort his own life out, isn't he?'

Maria nodded. 'There are plenty of local girls who'd jump at the chance of catching him. He's a good-looking man with character, but I've never noticed him that much interested in Elena — or anyone else, for that matter, even though he's very popular with the girls.'

Claire picked up some sanding paper and a piece of wood. 'Perhaps he simply hasn't met the right one yet. It'll all fall into place one day, I expect, and then you can plan the best wedding breakfast ever.'

'So, what do you think about Eduardo?'

Claire coloured at the question and she was glad she was bent over her work.

'Me? I think he's very polite and intelligent, and I like the way he's met the challenge of keeping the farm going. I don't know if family ties are stronger in Spain than they are in the UK, but I know some men who wouldn't feel responsible for someone else's past mistakes and they'd simply get up and go, to build a life of their own, somewhere else.'

Maria's shoulders straightened. 'Not Eduardo. He has too much Noriega blood in his veins. The Noriegas don't give up easily. What about you? Have you a sweetheart waiting for you when you go home?'

Claire laughed. 'No.'

Maria got to her feet and put her empty mug down. 'Well, that's enough gossiping for one day. I've lunch to get ready. It's a pity you don't join us, you could do with some more meat on your bones!'

Claire giggled. 'Don't you start, Maria. I am not too thin, and I am not hungry. I eat a big meal every evening — more here than I do at home. I tend to skip cooking if I'm tired and up to my eyes in work. A store-bought pizza and a salad is sometimes all I manage.'

Maria tutted and gave an exaggerated look of disapproval.

Claire shrugged her shoulders. 'I know. My mother nags me about 'decent meals' all the time. I do try, but you need time to cook properly and I don't always have time. One day, when I've lots of money, I'll plan things properly. I like cooking, and your food is wonderful. I'd like to take some of your recipes home with me, when I go.'

Maria gave her a toothy smile and nodded, gratified. She straightened her apron and went back to the main house.

Watching her, Claire saw how she picked up something that had fallen over and stood it against the wall. To Claire, the gesture showed how much she identified her whole being with the Noriega family. She wasn't just a household help; she was like a family member, who contributed to the wellbeing of the place in whatever small ways she could.

Claire liked her. She was completely down to earth and when they talked, Claire forgot that she was Spanish and of another generation. Maria's English was good, and her way of thinking was so direct and very endearing to Claire — Maria reminded her of her own grandmother, whose favourite maxim was 'you should call a spade a spade'.

Who knows what Maria could have achieved if she'd been born fifty years later? The intelligence and determination was there, but the possibilities open to women weren't so plentiful in those days.

* * *

Later that afternoon, Eduardo strolled in while Claire was admiring her own work. When she noticed him, she felt her pleasure growing. She'd finished and fitted the drawers, and the desk looked liked new.

He viewed her, and then the furniture. 'It's finished?'

'Yes, completely. What do you think? Are you happy with the result?' she asked.

He followed the direction of her eyes. 'Yes, I am. It looks really very good.'

Claire coloured. 'That's what I hoped that you'd say. It's dry now. Can you put it somewhere else, then I can concentrate on the next piece?'

'Of course. We'll put it straight into the study to replace my father's old desk.'

'You're going to use it?'

'Yes. It's okay to do so, I hope?'

Claire nodded. 'Of course. It was made to be a desk, and I'll be glad if it's used for its original purpose. Some people only want to show off antiques. I understand why they want to do so, but it's much nicer if the furniture does its original job.'

'Pablo and I will fetch it later. I'll have to clear my father's desk out of the way first and make room for it.'

'No hurry.'

He paused. 'I'm going into town. If you've finished here for the day, how about coming along for the ride? Or perhaps you need something and would like me to bring it back for you?'

Claire was caught on the hop and her heart hopped too. She knew she didn't want to miss the chance. 'Yes. I'd like to. Can I get some paint remover? I still have enough but I'd like some more, just in case.'

'There's a big DIY store on the outskirts of the next town,' he said. 'We can try there; they're bound to have something. They don't have specialist products, but I imagine that paint removers are generally run-of-the-mill, aren't they?'

'If I can, I'd like to read what's in it and if you're prepared to translate what I don't understand, I'm sure we'll be able to find find a suitable one.'

He nodded. 'I need to pick up something from the bank, and one or two things from the local ironmonger. The DIY store is not far from there.'

'Give me a couple of minutes to clean myself up.'

He smiled. 'Ten minutes?'

'Yes. That'll be fine.'

'I'll go and warn Pablo about moving the desk this evening. I'll meet you back by the house in ten minutes.'

She quickly washed, combed her

hair, put on some lipstick, and changed into a knee-length skirt and shirt blouse. She waited for him with her bag slung over her shoulder.

He whistled when he returned. 'That's what I call on the dot. I didn't honestly think you'd be ready in that short time.'

Claire laughed softly, basking in his approval.

Maria was watering the flowers in the tubs along the wall of the house when Eduardo drove past with Claire in the passenger seat. With a thoughtful little smile, she stopped and watched the car disappearing down the track leading to the farm.

* * *

Claire didn't want to admit it, but at this moment going to the DIY store with Eduardo was the best thing that had happened today. She enjoyed his company, and had a sensation of wellbeing whenever she was with him.

She didn't need to worry about what she said, or how she said it.

They called in at a nearby village first, where Eduardo wanted to pick up some spare parts for a farm machine. He'd pointed out places on the way there; the local church where he'd been christened, his junior school and the wall behind which he and his friends had smoked their first cigarettes . . . and were so sick that they vowed never to touch one again.

She got out to wait for him when he went inside to get the spare parts. On his return, she was leaning against the car lifting her face to the sun. The warmth lulled her, and she jumped when, returning quietly, he remarked, 'You look like a contented cat.'

She watched him store his purchase away in the boot. 'I feel like one,' she said. 'This sun is just right; I'm afraid I burn if it's too fierce.'

'It gets hotter in the summer but nothing as extreme as in the south.

Gran used to have problems sometimes, too; probably English skins are more sensitive. She tried to avoid sunlight as much as she could and she always used to wear a battered straw hat everywhere she went. Ready?'

'Of course.' She got back into the car. The radio played softly in the background when he started the engine and once they were on the road, Claire asked, 'Do you know if your gran was ever homesick?'

'Yes, I think so. Children don't understand these things, but I noticed that she was down in the dumps sometimes. She used to disappear to her cottage and my grandfather would join her. Sometimes they were gone for a few hours, sometimes overnight, or even longer. I really do think they loved each other very much and that he tried very hard to compensate and make her happy.'

Claire stared at his well-formed hands folded around the steering wheel. 'In those days travel wasn't so easy, was it? But she could still telephone the UK?'

'Yes, we had a telephone, but I can't remember Gran using it very much. It cost too much, I expect. I imagine there were times when she felt quite isolated. She had a sister who took care of things for her in the UK, but she probably felt helpless and frustrated at times.'

'Do you think she ever regretted coming to Spain?'

'I asked her that once and she said, 'Never! Wait until you fall in love — nothing else has more significance or is more important.''

'It sounds as if she was a very interesting woman.'

'She was; interesting, intelligent, wise and very loving. My mother reminds me of her sometimes.'

He kept his eyes on the winding, sunlit road, but nevertheless Claire could hear the depth of feeling in his voice.

She enjoyed watching the scenery

and felt herself relaxing. 'I like the local countryside,' she commented happily. 'I never expected it to be hilly — or so green.' Looking into the distance through the windscreen, she commented, 'You even have snow-tipped mountains.'

'Most people think Spain is just a vast sun-drenched plain. Things do dry out in the summer, like everywhere else, but the heat isn't extreme and springtime and autumn are lovely. Those mountains you see are only an hour away by car, so we can go skiing in winter. Can you ski?'

'I went with the sixth form once and took a beginner's course. I'm not sure if I could even stay upright now — it was so long ago.'

He looked across and gave her a soft smile that sent something inside fluttering. 'I'm sure you haven't forgotten everything. It's like riding a bike; you never completely forget how, once you've learned.'

'Do you?' she asked him tentatively.

'Go skiing in the winter months, I mean?'

'Now and then. I'm not passionate about it. I enjoy golf more when I have the time, but I enjoy a day out in the mountains when it's quiet around the farm.'

He exited off the main road, drove down a side road, crossed a railway line and turned into an industrial estate, then parked in front of an impressive DIY centre.

Claire mused that these stores all looked the same all over the world. This one was painted in bright red and white and it was vast. She fell in step with Eduardo and he asked at the information desk where they could find paint remover. Taking her by the elbow, he said, 'Along here.'

They walked down the main gangway and turned off into a side aisle, one offering paints, varnishes and the like. Claire started to look for the kind of stripper she wanted.

Eduardo was slightly startled when

Claire began to read the labels, which were in Spanish, French or Italian. But she was checking the list of the chemicals because some had contents that could cause damage to old wood.

'This looks all right to me,' she said. 'It contains methylene chloride — that's important.'

He took it from her hand. 'Well, it's a paint remover. All the rest is double Dutch to me.'

'I try to stick to brands I know, but if I need to use this, I'll try it out on a hidden spot first.' Claire spotted a collection of quality brushes and began to handle them.

'I don't want to sound derisive.' Eduardo smiled. 'But a DIY centre is hardly the most exciting place to be . . . and yet you're quite fascinated by all of this, aren't you?'

'I like wandering around building shops and DIY stores in the same way that you probably love going to horse fairs.'

He laughed and his eyes twinkled.

'Fair enough, but let's leave any other purchases for another day. I'd prefer to invite you to share a cup of coffee and some Spanish cheesecake.'

'Cheesecake?' She smiled. 'My absolute favourite — I'll even leave the DIY for that!'

'Good. Let's pay for your pot of methylene thing-me-bob, and be on our way, then.'

Claire now knew roughly where to find the store, and she didn't need to speak Spanish to wander around or to pay at the cash desk. She intended to come back and take a proper look at it all later, but for the moment going somewhere to spend time with Eduardo was much more enticing even than gathering restoration materials.

With a spring in her step, she followed him back to the car and he drove on for a while before turning off the main road to join a smaller one.

Soon after, he pulled up in front of a small café with a few tables located on the pavement outside. The street was quiet and the blue and white checked tablecloths danced in the soft breeze. There was a middle-aged couple at one of the tables and Eduardo greeted them politely as he led the way to a corner table. There was a large, leafy tree growing directly alongside the wall and it provided some welcome shade. Claire knew that it was a fig tree; she'd seen several before, and always admired the large leaves.

A plump woman with dangling earrings, wearing a spotless white apron, bustled out with a pencil and pad in her hand. Seeing Eduardo, she smiled broadly and chatted away in Spanish with machine-gun precision. He must have told her who Claire was, because the woman eyed her thoughtfully before she smiled at Claire, and Claire smiled back. She continued to chat to Eduardo, took their order, and hurried indoors.

Eduardo leaned back and stretched his hands behind his head, sticking his long legs out in a straight line. He explained, 'Isabelle is the mother of an old school friend of mine. I've been coming here on my own or with others as long as I can remember. She makes wonderful cakes.'

'It's a long way from the farm, isn't it?' Claire asked. 'How did you get here?'

'With the school bus, by bike, or later by scooter, or car. Julio has a couple of brothers; I was part of their crowd when we were growing up.'

'Did you wish you had a brother?'

He shrugged. 'Perhaps . . . but not really. I never had time to be bored. Julio was one of my best friends, but we drifted apart a little when I went to boarding school in England, and later when I was at university and he moved away to train for his job. But we somehow managed to keep in touch and have stayed friends.'

Isabelle came back with a loaded tray and spread everything with practised ease. The coffee was aromatic and the cheesecake melted in her mouth when Claire tasted it.

'Umm! This is terrific. She ought to get a mention in a travel brochure.'

Cup in hand, Eduardo said thoughtfully, 'Isabelle isn't interested in making huge profits. She's always put her family first. The income from the café helped swell the family budget, but she's never wanted to expand. Julio is a surveyor in Barcelona now, so I don't see him very often. I keep in touch through Isabelle, and when he's home with his wife and family I always drop in. I almost feel like part of the family.'

Claire said, 'It sounds like a solid friendship.'

He nodded.

Claire looked around at the quiet street and up at the large-leafed branches of the trees moving in the warm breeze. 'This is just perfect,' she sighed.

'Isabelle enjoys running the café. She hears all the news, she has dozens of contacts, and everyone knows her.' He shifted in his seat. 'And do you have friends, special friends . . . perhaps even a boyfriend?'

'Yes, yes, and no. I grew up on the outskirts of a town, so there was probably a lot more going on for me than for you. It was easier for me to find things to do. My father was strict, but as long as he approved of where I went and who I went with, it was fine. Friendship is difficult to analyse, isn't it? I did have a very good friend; we were always together. Unfortunately for me, she moved to the north of Scotland when she married a few years ago. We keep in touch, but it's not the same; I miss her. She's happy and she married a lovely man, so I'm glad for her. I know lots of other people, and I enjoy my work, and my life.'

'So, no steady boyfriend?'

Her body language told him she was at ease with the question. 'No. The right person hasn't come along, and as I don't believe in playing around just for fun, I'm in danger of ending up as a spinster of the parish.'

He eyed her thoughtfully. 'Finding the right partner isn't always easy, is it? Especially if you don't want to compromise.'

Claire shook her head and mused that she felt very comfortable with this man, even though he was someone she hardly knew. 'What's the point in getting married unless you're absolutely sure? It would be a disaster to marry for the wrong reasons.'

'Agreed.' He smiled easily. 'Maria has been trying to marry me off ever since I came back from university.'

Claire laughed and tilted her head to the side. 'Yes, so I've noticed,' she said.

'She's probably very frustrated because I'm sure she's thinking that the farm needs the next generation.' He shrugged. 'Perhaps she's right, but getting married just to provide the place with an heir is a pretty dismal prospect in this day and age. It worked in past centuries when people married to increase their power and riches. But perhaps Alisa or Antonio will develop a passion for the place and their bachelor uncle will stand back and hand it over.'

'You're not exactly in your dotage yet — and you are a good catch. Maria told me so herself.'

He grinned. 'Did she? Trust Maria! I don't want to be a good catch; I'd rather be someone who's worth knowing.'

Claire coloured when she said, 'Well, be reassured, you're that too.' She took a sip from her coffee cup. It rattled a little as she put it back in the saucer. 'What a lovely break. Thank you for this.'

'You're welcome. I thought that you'd enjoy an interruption from your work. You do keep your nose to the grindstone rather a lot, don't you?'

'That's the pot calling the kettle black,' she observed. 'I don't see you lounging around much, either.'

'There's always something to do on a farm. It never ends. It's very interesting, though. The other day Maria suggested we could grow fruit of some kind and make jam on a commercial scale; it's not a bad idea. People are keen on home-produced products these days. I'm still thinking about what's involved — and I still have some other ideas I'd like to try out, as soon as our income is stable.'

'You didn't mind — becoming a farmer, I mean?'

'I didn't train to be a farmer, but it was always at the back of my mind. As I don't have a brother, and my sister never showed any interest, I knew it would eventually fall into my lap. I've learned a lot in the last couple of years, from local farmers, from books, and from people like Pablo who know the area and have a lifetime of experience of what will function, or not.' He looked at his watch. 'I want to call at the bank on the way back, so if you don't mind . . . '

She gulped the remains of her coffee. 'No, of course not. Why didn't you say something earlier?'

He chuckled. 'I didn't mean that you have to toss it down like that. Take your time.'

She brushed the side of her jeans. 'No, I'm ready, honestly. Let's go.'

'Spanish banks are very strict about closing times, and I've an appointment with the manager because they have longer hours this afternoon. It's the only day in the week they do.'

He got up and took some money out of his wallet, shoving it under his plate, then turned to Claire and explained. 'When we say goodbye to Isabelle she won't take any money, she never has, but I outsmart her!'

Claire waited while he disappeared into the shadows of the café. Isabelle emerged with him a few minutes later and said something to her in Spanish.

Claire looked at Eduardo, and he obliged. 'She said she hopes to see you again soon.'

The older woman's eyes were kind and Claire at least managed, 'Gracias!'

and a smile before she turned and hurried out after Eduardo who was already getting into the car.

She'd enjoyed her trip with him. He was a private kind of man, but she'd learned a lot about him in an afternoon, and she liked him a lot; liked his friendly attitude. She didn't know if he had ever thought about the kiss on the beach. She had . . . but she didn't intend to bring it up, ever.

On their way, they passed a bright red Mini and the driver hooted at them. Claire noticed Elena and Juan inside. Elena gave them a wave as they passed, but she didn't look pleased.

It was too late to start working again when they got back, so Claire spent some time playing hopscotch with Alisa for a while before they went to feed the ducks again.

Later, Pablo and Eduardo came to collect the desk. It now had a beautiful patina and shone a rich golden colour as the two men carried it across the yard and into the house. Claire felt proud of her work; she always did when she knew it had been a job well done.

That evening Maria and Sophia Noriega were full of praise when they all went to look at the desk, now positioned in front of the window in a book-lined study. It looked just as if it belonged there.

The meal was pleasant and as delicious as always, and Claire was contented when she returned to her cottage and picked up her paperback. She hadn't seen a television programme or read a newspaper for days, and she didn't miss them. Mrs Noriega had mentioned a couple of times that they had satellite reception with English TV channels and she was welcome to join them. But Claire didn't want to interfere with their choice and was quite happy to be in her own company at the end of the day.

5

Maria had made a fish soup, and it was excellent. Eduardo had two helpings and looked slightly surprised when Maria said she didn't have any more. During the meal, they chatted about the new priest and various other local happenings.

Claire noted that Eduardo often dodged questions about what he was doing in his spare time. His mother asked thoughtfully, and with care, while Maria was more forthright in her questioning; Eduardo smiled and side-stepped them both.

She could understand why; there was a real danger that their ideas and lifestyle would overrun his own. He needed room to breathe, to choose his own friends and interests, away from the farm. Maria had already told her that he had a circle of friends, played golf whenever he got the chance, and was well known for his riding skills and the horses he bred. This evening he disappeared without explanation soon after Maria had finished serving them coffee and some sweet cake.

Claire accepted the two women's invitation to join them watching the television. They chose a British station for her benefit and they all watched the latest episode of Inspector Barnaby while sharing a bottle of red wine and some salted almonds. Maria knitted furiously and Sophia Noriega and Claire commented on the happenings. It was a very comfortable evening and Claire admitted she'd enjoyed herself.

She liked both women. She knew that Mrs Noriega handled the book-keeping and most of the office work. She was as passionate about the farm as her son was, but didn't show it until she knew a person quite well.

By the time Claire went back to the cottage, the moon was a silver disc, and the night air was cool, but not unpleasant. If the farm hadn't been completely blanketed in darkness, she'd have been tempted to go for a walk in the moonlight.

* * *

Juan came calling again next morning. Claire had just established that she'd run out of the right grade of sandpaper and was about to see if she could find the DIY centre on her own. Her heart sank when she saw him walking towards the barn. She began arming herself with excuses before his shadow had even crossed the threshold. If nothing, he was a determined character, she thought ruefully.

He appraised, and evidently approved of, her linen trousers and lightweight silk sweater. 'Hi! How's things going? What about our date?'

Claire smiled thinly. 'We don't have a date, Juan — and you know that.'

He looked at her wickedly. 'That's what I mean. Come out with me and then I promise to leave you alone.'

Claire placed her hands on her hips. 'I don't understand you. You're not really interested in me, are you? You're only interested in making another conquest.'

He grinned. 'Perhaps. You were out with Eduardo yesterday. What's he got that I haven't?'

Sounding a little exasperated, she explained. 'Eduardo took me to the DIY centre because I needed some stuff for stripping.'

'I'd be glad to come and see you stripping any day.'

Claire rolled her eyes. 'Don't be silly, Juan, you know what I mean. I was getting materials for my work.'

He laughed loudly when he saw her colour rise. 'How quaint you are — the merest hint of impropriety and you blush.' He took a step forward and Claire took a step back. She turned her head to the side when he made a move to touch her head. His colour rose slightly and his eyes suddenly had a sharper expression in their depths.

'Stop that, Juan! You may not have anything useful to do, but I have. In fact, I'm on my way to the DIY store again because I need more sandpaper. Do you know what that is?'

He nodded eagerly. 'But of course. I'll take you.'

Claire wished he would leave. 'No, thanks. I know where it is, and how to get there. I won't waste your time and anyway I'm positive you would be bored to death waiting for me.' Claire was fed up with being polite. 'I like browsing around. I would imagine a DIY centre is the last place you'd want to be stuck in for long.'

He shrugged and looked injured. 'You're a hard person to win over. You don't know what you're missing.' He considered her a moment. 'Are you sure you know how to get there?'

Claire recited the way as she remembered it.

He nodded. 'Okay, but if you branch off at the side road, opposite the church, and drive straight on, you'll save yourself a couple of miles. It ends in view of that railway crossing near the DIY. The way is rougher, but you have a Jeep.'

Trying to be pleasant, she nodded. 'Okay, I'll try it. Thanks.'

He lifted his hand and turned on his heel. Claire was surprised that he'd abandoned his endeavour to win her over for a date so easily, but she was relieved too. Once he'd disappeared from sight, she collected the keys of the Jeep and set off.

* * *

It was a straightforward drive until she reached the church. She recognised it from afar and slowed down when she came closer. There was little traffic about so she didn't block anyone else on the road. Drawing to a halt near the church, she looked around. She spotted the side road Juan had mentioned and didn't think twice.

The prospect of driving down a quiet country track was much more enticing than following the main road. The way was overgrown, but easy to follow and it was no problem for her Jeep. It was a bright day full of sunshine and as she drove along there were fringes of a little wood on one side and wild greenery on the other. She met no one along the way, so she had time to view the sprouting ferns and listen to the rattling and scaling of small stones when she drove over patches of them as she drove along contentedly.

The way twisted and curved. There was suddenly a fork in the road and she slowed down. Juan had said straight on, so she went on. The way climbed in a shallow curve and the Jeep automatically picked up speed when she reached the top and began to descend on the other side. She was captivated by her surroundings, and some bright flowering bushes that bordered the way caught her attention.

It was sheer luck that she looked up

at the right moment and noticed that the road suddenly seemed to disappear. She braked abruptly, and the screech cut through the silence as she steered the Jeep sideways onto the grass verge. Thrusting the door open quickly she got out, feeling the thorns of some straggly bushes on her bare legs as she did so. She fought her way forward for about twenty yards and found that the road ended with no warning and just a rotten fence. There was a drop of at least fifty feet into a disused quarry.

She shuddered, thinking about what could have happened if she'd been speeding and not paying enough attention.

Once she'd calmed down, she couldn't ignore the question that was hammering in her head — had Juan sent her along this road deliberately, or had she misunderstood and taken the wrong direction when the road forked? It was silly to think that Juan wished her evil; not even he would do something as wicked as that just because she refused to go out with him, surely? She made her way back to the Jeep, thanking her lucky stars. She leaned against the side and took a drink from a bottle she always carried with her. She reversed carefully, and followed the track back. Reaching the fork, she no longer felt like exploring, so she carried on and joined the main road again.

Still feeling a little shocked, she visited the store and spent some time wandering the gangways and comparing prices and quality. By the time she'd made her purchases, she'd almost forgotten what had happened.

Claire saw some delicious-looking pastries in a shop and, pointing and smiling, she managed to make the saleswoman understand. With a paper tray full of pastries on the passenger seat next to her, she made her way home again. She went into the kitchen and presented Maria with her acquisitions.

Maria beamed. Probably she seldom ate pastries she hadn't made herself, and it would be a treat for her.

'They look good. Señora Noriega is in the living room. Please go on through while I make us some tea, and we'll soon get rid of this lot!'

Sophia Noriega was reading a book and she looked up when Claire came in. Claire explained why she was here and Sophia patted the chair by her side. 'That was thoughtful. We don't spoil Maria enough. Come and sit down.'

After a few generalities, Claire told her about branching off down the wrong track. Sophia Noriega's hand flew to her mouth. 'Claire! You could have been killed or badly injured. What was Juan thinking of, to send you there? Hardly anyone uses the shortcut any more; it is too overgrown. If you'd forked off to the right, you would have eventually come out near the railway track but the other track only leads to the disused old quarry. Are you sure you understood him properly?'

Claire shrugged as Maria came in

and started to arrange the tea things. Sophia told her what had happened and Maria looked rather angry.

'Juan is trouble with a capital T.' She handed Claire a plate and a cup of tea. 'Why didn't he take you himself?'

'He wanted to, but I didn't want him along.'

Biting into a soft pastry, Maria commented, 'I can understand that. That boy is going to end up in real trouble one day. I can't understand how a nice person like Philip De Silva can have a son like Juan.'

* * *

Eduardo came across to the barn later that afternoon. He'd obviously come straight from the fields; he was covered in dust and clad in faded jeans and a blue work shirt. His working boots looked heavy and cumbersome although she guessed they were lightweight and practical. His gaze was riveted on her face at first, then moved over her slowly. Her heart jolted and her pulse pounded out of control.

'Maria just told me about your near-miss. Are you all right?'

Breathless, she could only look at him and nod.

He pushed his hands into his pockets. 'Juan is an idiot!'

Claire didn't want to cause any more animosity. She was sure she hadn't misunderstood Juan, but she had no intention of telling Eduardo so. She wasn't sure how he would react.

'No more than I am for going down a little-used track without checking and knowing where I was,' she said apologetically.

One hand snaked out of his pocket and he reached forward to trace the side of her cheek. Claire had to steady her pulse and will herself not to react visibly to his touch. Prickles of excitement swept over her skin.

'As long as you didn't get hurt, that's the main thing,' he said softly. 'See you later?'

'Yes, of course.'

She tried in vain to read his features, before he turned away and went towards the house again.

6

Usually Eduardo was around the farmhouse first thing, until he'd sorted out any immediate problems that needed his attention. After that he disappeared to work on whatever was on his schedule for that day. He was always busy and often she could guess where he was, by the sound of the farm machinery or by hammering sounds somewhere in one of the distant fields.

The neighbourhood was fundamentally very peaceful. The air was clear and very fresh this morning and, strengthened by some fragrant coffee, Claire concentrated on her work again.

Mid-afternoon she heard the familiar tap on the doorframe. She looked up, smiled, pushed the errant curls from her face and walked towards him.

They came face-to-face, and a pleasing smell of grasses and plants swirled around in the breeze.

'Everything okay?' Eduardo asked.

'I'm fine, thanks.' She hoped he wouldn't notice, but for some stupid reason seeing him was making her feel confused. Suddenly, she realised — she was falling in love with him.

His dark eyebrows slanted and he waited silently. He was still in his working gear and he stood tall and straight, black hair gleaming in the sunshine.

Despite the fact that he wasn't making the slightest effort to make an impression, there was something about Eduardo that electrified her more than she wanted to admit.

The reaction made her feel slightly silly. She said quickly, 'Don't bother about yesterday; perhaps I did misunderstand.'

He removed his working glove from one hand and ran it over his face. His expression was more serious, his voice was calm, and his gaze was steady.

'Juan and I were never close friends

and what happened yesterday hasn't improved my opinion of him. I feel sorry for Philip, because he somehow manages to keep the farm functioning. Juan could lighten the burden, but he prefers to fritter his time away on other things, including women.' He gave a gruff laugh. 'Just carry on with your work, Claire and try to ignore him. But if he bothers you again, please do not hesitate to tell me.'

'I don't want to cause any trouble.'

'You can't help being an eye-catching woman, Claire. Juan presumes he's entitled to anyone wearing a skirt that comes within reach.'

With tongue in cheek, Claire said, 'Until yesterday, I'd never worn a skirt when he was around.'

Eduardo laughed. 'See what happens when you do?' He put his hands on his hips, looking comfortable with himself. 'I've promised to take the kids for a walk before dinner. Would you like to come? I could show you Gran's cottage, if you'd like.'

She smiled. 'Yes, actually, I would like that.'

'See you in thirty minutes or so, then? I need a shower and a change of clothes first.'

'So do I.'

His brows lifted and he gave her a crooked smile that sent her pulse soaring on wings. They smiled at each other before he turned away.

Claire hurried back to the cottage. It was a sheer pleasure to soak in a scented bath for a while. When she heard the children, she went out to join the others with shining hair, three-quarter length white jeans and a wrap-around V-necked red top.

* * *

It was a lovely day. Eduardo, Claire and the children set off. They went towards the hill, and paused at the pond for Alisa to feed her duck.

Claire noticed the pond wasn't quite as full as the day she first saw it, although there was still plenty of water; there must be a spring somewhere supplying it. Some wild birds were swimming lazily among the reeds on the far side. Eduardo knelt down, talking to Alisa, and Claire watched them for a while. When the paper bag was empty, they all set off again and Eduardo joined her while the children ran ahead.

The tantalising smell of his freshly washed skin drifted towards her on the breeze. It was so good to be out in the fresh air, and to be with him. They went straight on; she was suddenly aware of the outlines of a small cottage in the distance and she realised they were within reach of his grandmother's hideaway. Claire was curious to see what it was like.

When they were close enough, she saw that although it needed some attention, the walls looked solid and it was clearly not in danger of falling apart. The grey-layered stonework was firm and the deep-set window-niches had wrought-iron bars. The downstairs windows had closed wooden shutters. It was a romantic, remote spot. She stepped back and looked up. The thick stone slates on the roof still seemed to be effectively protecting the cottage from rain and storm. A tiny dormer-like window was set into the eaves.

Claire strolled away from the others and circled the building, avoiding the nettles and the brambles. There were faint remains of a kind of flowerbed along one wall. It had probably been a favourite spot for Eduardo's grandmother to sit and relax. Silence reigned, apart from the sound of sheep bleating close at hand. Above her, wild birds were flying in an untidy formation; they flapped their wings in silent unison as they sailed across the blue sky.

When she returned to Eduardo, he'd already opened the front door. The children were inside; she could hear them chatting somewhere. He motioned her forwards. A musty odour wafted towards them. The children were upstairs; their footsteps echoed on the planking. She hovered in the doorway and then stepped gingerly onto the flagged floor ahead of Eduardo. The door to her left opened into what must have been a kitchen; she could just about make out the outlines of an old-fashioned porcelain sink beneath the window in the gloom.

The door to her right opened into a slightly larger room and Claire imagined that it had probably been some kind of living room. She crossed to one of the windows. With a struggle she wrenched the inner casement open and then pushed the wooden shutters outwards. Light flooded the room. She turned and saw Eduardo looking around nostalgically. The room contained only a few pieces of discarded, shabby furniture that was clearly of no value.

She wandered back through the musty rooms and opened all the wooden shutters. Light flooded the place; the clean air was a definite improvement on the decayed atmosphere it replaced. Looking out from one of the windows across the surrounding countryside, she saw the silhouette of a lone rider on the crest of a hill.

The protective measures on the windows were logical; the cottage had never been in continuous use, even by Eduardo's grandmother, so the wrought iron bars were intended to make sure that no uninvited stranger got in. She climbed the steep wooden stairs, holding on tightly to the banister in case any of the steps were rotten. The children were staring out of the unshuttered window and pointing out landmarks they knew. She looked around briefly and then went back downstairs, her sandals clattering as she went. Eduardo was standing at one of the windows.

'It's a nice little cottage,' she said warmly. 'It's safe, and in good structural condition.'

He shrugged. 'It looked even better

when Gran lived here. It's surprising how curtains, carpets and the like improve a place like this. It seemed very romantic to me as a kid, but today I just think that it would be very impractical to live here. Water from a well, no electricity.'

'Your grandmother came from a different generation. We've got used to the blessings of modern society, but in those days lots of people lived in cottages like this all their lives.'

It was already late afternoon and quite warm outside, but inside it was much colder. The cottage had thick walls and flagged stone floors. She looked at the solid walls and half-empty rooms and thought about the Englishwoman who'd lived here. She'd been cut off from her homeland and made herself a small refuge, surrounded by furniture that reminded her of her origins. 'I can imagine that with a lot of care and a bit of imaginative decoration, it could be quite pretty again.'

Eduardo strode around, closing the shutters again. 'I'll have to think carefully about doing it up. It'll cost a lot — and who's going to use it?'

He shouted up the steep staircase. 'Alisa . . . Antonio, come on, we're leaving now.'

The children's feet clattered on the steps and they ran straight outside.

Eduardo waited until Claire was out and pulled the door behind him firmly. He attached the padlock and locked it with one of the keys on his keyring. 'There's a spare key under that large boulder over there,' he remarked. 'That's where Gran left it, the last time she was here.'

Without a backward glance, he walked towards the children on the edge of the field. Claire followed.

Antonio had brought a Frisbee along and the two children began to play. Claire joined in and enjoyed herself almost as much as the two youngsters. The field had sweet-smelling grass spotted with poppies and some small blue flowers that Claire didn't recognise.

They'd been playing for a while when Claire noticed Eduardo was still watching them, sitting astride the fence.

She called across, 'Come and join us.'

He gave an exaggerated groan of exhaustion. 'After a long, hard day's work?'

'We've all had a hard day's work. That's no excuse.'

Alisa and Antonio chorused as one. 'Yes, come on!'

He jumped down and strode across to them, saying humorously, 'There's no peace for the wicked, is there?'

Claire wished her heartbeat didn't act so erratically whenever he was around. He took up position and they began throwing to each other again. The children tried to out-trick him, but they didn't succeed.

Claire decided she'd try to hoodwink him too. She aimed and succeeded in making him run, but he understood the challenge and made her run more, too.

It turned into a competition of the fittest she couldn't win.

They didn't cut the children out of the fun but tempered the distances they threw for them, eyeing each other with mischief in their eyes. Claire found herself moving automatically further away whenever it was his turn to throw and hers to catch. She felt light-headed. He showed her no mercy. She was forced to make a belly-flop, determined to catch it before it hit the ground. His laughter only made her more single-minded.

All of them were soon out of breath, but it was fun. Alisa and Antonio were reluctant to stop, and were soon playing on the other side of the hedge. They could hear them, but not see them. Eduardo sat down in the grass and plucked at a stalk of grass. He was in an exuberant mood.

Claire joined him, feeling that it would be okay to sit down next to him. The silence around them and the field full of fragrant grass and wild flowers had a heady effect. She didn't trust herself to speak as her awareness of him grew. Supporting herself on her hands behind her back, her head tipped towards the sun, she looked at him and forced lightness into her voice when she said, 'This is a great place to be. Just smell the grass and the clean air!'

He laughed and looked at her indulgently. 'You are mad. You can smell clean air?'

The feeling of nearness and camaraderie was overwhelming and she cleared her throat trying not to appear affected. 'You know what I mean.'

There was a flicker in his eyes and then they roamed over her figure. He nodded. 'Yes, I think I do.'

She studied the now-familiar tanned face and tried to assess his unreadable features. When his gaze met hers, her heart turned over. She lost control of her thoughts. He threw away the blade of grass and leaned towards her, leaving her no room to breathe, and did what she had been longing for him to do.

His lips met hers fiercely and she responded, wanting more, running her hands through his hair as his arm slid around her back to clasp her to him. Her mind ceased functioning and his nearness kindled feelings of fire that made her senses spin.

Now his lips were just out of reach and she yearned for him to kiss her again, more than anything she'd wanted before. Just the thought of it tied a knot in her stomach.

It was a second, but it could have been an eternity. The atmosphere was full of something unpredictable and just a whisker away from the inevitable.

For a long moment Eduardo stared into her face, his dark eyes burning. Then he released her, rose to his feet in an effortless movement, straightened abruptly, and moved a step away from her.

'I'm sorry — I shouldn't have done that. I'm in no position to begin any kind of relationship with anyone.'

Claire's breath was too fast and her

cheeks were too warm. She strove to bring her longing under control and to conceal the world-shaking effect he was having on her, standing with his legs apart, looking down at her. The tension between them hadn't lessened.

She scrambled to her feet, too. He was still too close for her emotions to settle but when she noticed that he was scowling at her, or at himself, it suddenly helped to steady her nerves. Claire noticed his fists were in a tight ball. He said in a constrained voice through tight lips, 'I'll find the children. It's about time to finish the game.' He spun on his heel and strode off, leaving her crestfallen and bewildered.

Claire watched him as he strode determinedly away. She wondered what he meant by not being in a position to follow his instincts. Did it perhaps mean he'd made some kind of promise to Elena, even though he felt attracted to her? She looked unseeingly towards the distant mountains. The journey back to the farmhouse was silent. The children's noisy chatter filled the gap and helped Claire concentrate on something other than the tall, dark man with his stiff expression.

* * *

That evening at dinner, she still felt awkward, and although Eduardo was quiet, no one else noticed because he was always more of a listener than a chatterer. She followed his lead. His square jaw was tense and Claire wasn't sure if she should try to iron out the situation at the next best opportunity — or not . . . but how could she? Although he attracted her more than any man she'd ever met before, he clearly didn't feel the same about her and he didn't want to get involved.

Mere physical attraction was not real love; she knew that, but it wasn't just his physical desirability that was turning her life upside down. There was more to it than that; she was in love with the man, and everything that he stood for.

She sat outside her cottage later, watched the red and gold sun vanishing behind the horizon before the darkness of the evening took over. She decided to concentrate on her work — and leave tomorrow, and every day thereafter, to fate.

* * *

Although the morning seemed to pass quickly and she was making progress, Claire's concentration wasn't as it should be and, in the end, she decided to stop and go for a walk. Being on her own and walking along the edges of the lonely fields was strangely comforting.

Even if she felt confused about Eduardo and worried about how she was going to extract herself out of this situation without a broken heart, she didn't regret coming to Spain for a moment.

It was a bright, sunny day and there were breezes filled with scents of the pastures and of the salty sea far away.

The blue sky with its scudding clouds presented a perfect image for a talented artist. She was happy to be here.

She climbed the ridge of a hill slowly and felt the sun on her face. Looking down, she could see a scattering of Eduardo's cattle in one of the fields. They looked like miniature toys; only these particular toys were moving, and she knew they were anything but miniatures.

She observed them idly for a few minutes. She'd seen them before often, sometimes at very close quarters on the other side of a hedge; they were cream in colour and had long horns. Eduardo had mentioned that they were some special breed.

As far as Claire was concerned, they were cattle, animals she knew nothing about, that looked rather huge and fierce.

She wasn't a child of the countryside and knew nothing about livestock. Whenever she was out walking round Casona de la Esquina, she tried to avoid any fields where she thought they would be grazing.

Here, clinging to the side of the hill, and basking in the afternoon sun, there were neat lines of vegetables in a well-tended field — and Claire noticed that the cattle seemed to be meandering towards it.

Her eyes glided along the perimeter hedges until she found the gate, which was wide open. She was startled, scared by the knowledge that it was up to her to find a quick solution. She realised that she had to do something before the cattle trampled the plants into the ground and chewed up part of Eduardo's annual earnings. It could only be a matter of minutes until one of them spotted the gap — and as soon as one found the way, the others would follow!

Biting her lip, Claire tried to think straight. She rubbed her hands on her jeans and felt a lump. Her telephone! Normally she kept her phone in her handbag, but she'd pushed it into her pocket when she was working in the barn.

She remembered that she had Eduardo's number stored on her list from before she left England. She fumbled in the pocket of her jeans and nervously punched the buttons, searching her contacts, until she found his name.

It rang several times and she mumbled loudly to herself, willing him to answer. She almost gave up, and then she heard his voice.

'Hello?'

'Eduardo? This is Claire,' she said breathlessly.

'Claire? Where are you? Why are you phoning me?' He registered the agitated concern in her voice and asked, 'What's the matter?'

'I'm up in a field looking down on your cattle. They are about to get into a neighbouring field full of vegetables. The gate is open, and I don't know what to do. I'm scared of them!'

'Field, which field?'

'I don't know. I'm out for a walk and just happened to spot the cows, they're on the move and en route for your veggies. What can I do?'

He chortled. 'Claire, they are not cows, they are cattle. I know where the cattle were this morning . . . the vegetables — they have spindly stalks, and a bunch of leaves on top?'

'Yes. What shall I do?'

'Right, yes, I know where you are. I'm in another field, not very far away from you. Don't worry — I'll be with you in a couple of minutes.'

Claire looked back towards the field and suddenly screeched.

'Claire! Claire? What's the matter?'

'The first one is almost at the gate. I'll have to try to chase him off.'

She heard him laughing softly, before she stuck the phone back in her pocket and began to run helter-skelter down between the rows of vegetables towards the gate.

She almost stumbled in the loose earth a couple of times, but it was a race between her and the leading animal. She was determined these cattle weren't going to make Eduardo's life more difficult than it was already.

Gathering all her courage round her like a cloak, and trying not to think about the size of the animals' horns, she ran on.

The hungry beast was drawing closer to the gate, but so was she. Claire could see the other animals beginning to take interest and starting to gather behind the first one.

If she didn't succeed and the leading animal got through the gap, there was a good chance the herd would trample her.

She sprinted the last couple of yards, headed straight for the side of the gate and dragged it across, pushing it in front of her and almost slamming it on the nose of the poor advancing animal. It made a clanging sound as it fell into the lock.

The beast looked shocked, and made a loud, affronted racket. It gazed hungrily at the vegetables it had almost tasted.

Claire moved back from the gate and waited.

She heard the sound of a tractor, and then she saw it opening a pathway through the cattle towards the gate. Eduardo jumped down and mounted the gate easily, shoving the leading animal aside to do so.

Landing with a thud on the other side, he came towards her laughing, his arms held open. 'Come here.'

She went. She went to Eduardo, and to safety.

He picked her up and swung her around before setting her down gently, gazing at her face and then kissing her softly. Finally he crushed her close to him for an all-too-short moment.

'You are absolutely amazing,' he told her. 'You're scared to death of those creatures, and you still think you have to save my vegetables?'

With joy bubbling up inside and her heart beating like a locomotive on the move, she looked up at his amused face.

Gathering her senses again, she finally spluttered, 'You know you can't afford to lose those vegetables, and I must correct you — they are not 'poor animals'. They are very big, very heavy and only have one thing on their mind — eating.'

He threw back his head and laughed, still holding her close.

He kissed her quickly on her forehead and threw an arm round her shoulder as he propelled her towards the gate.

He swept an arc through the air with his hand and made an elaborate bow.

'My heartfelt thanks for saving my vegetables. Come on, I'll take you back to the farm on my tractor.'

He helped her over the gate and warily she accompanied him past the cattle that were chewing and viewing them curiously, but passively.

He mounted the tractor and gave her a hand up to a small side-seat next to his. Revving the engine, they set off across the field, scattering the cattle as they bounced along.

Claire had the feeling that a ride in a Silver Cloud Rolls Royce along a highway into the sunset couldn't have been more exhilarating.

* * *

Claire went over to the main house for the evening meal, and greeted everyone as usual.

The two women eyed her with interest, and then Maria chortled. 'Eduardo told us about your adventure with the cattle.'

Claire coloured. 'I was only trying to save his vegetables. If everyone is going to make fun of the fact that I don't like cattle, next time I will leave the herd to do what they like with the blasted vegetables!'

Maria started to laugh and lifted her apron to wipe her eyes. She waved her hands in the air. 'No, we all know you don't like them and are scared of them, it was very commendable. Come and sit down. It is so funny, we have beef and vegetables for dinner this evening!'

The two women looked at Claire and started to laugh again. Claire waited a moment and then she joined in with them.

Eduardo, already sitting at the table, grinned. His dark eyes sparkled as he watched her sit down. They talked about a local religious festival that was due in a couple of weeks, and Claire listened with interest. She mused regretfully that she'd be gone by then.

Eduardo pushed back his chair after finishing his coffee. 'I've got to muck out the stables. I might go down the golf club for an hour later on. I haven't been there for a while.'

Claire remained seated for longer, enjoying another last cup of coffee. She knew by now there was always an unspoken invitation to stay and watch the television whenever she felt like it, so she stayed.

* * *

She was up early. She enjoyed lazing in bed sometimes but, on other days like today, she woke naturally early enough to watch the darkness surrender to the kinder colours of the morning sunrise. The air seemed particularly pure and fresh first thing, and there was a wonderful feeling of a new beginning to each morning.

She was free to work undisturbed. The first wave of morning sunshine was beginning to push up the temperature by the time a familiar knock on the framework made her look up. As she hoped, it was Eduardo. Her heart pounded out of control.

'Good morning.'

'Hi.' She smiled.

'Want a ride on the tractor again? I'm going up to the top field.'

She shook her head and laughed. 'I presume you're going past the cattle again. I've better things to do.'

He shrugged and grinned. 'Pity, I

thought you enjoyed our little trip yesterday and would be prepared to face the dangers, just to be with me.' He turned on his heel and lifted his hand in a wave as he went.

She listened to him whistling softly to himself as he crossed the yard and disappeared for the morning's work.

Claire sighed and turned back to her work again. Much as she would have relished spending time with him, and her heart thrilled with the knowledge that he seemed to feel the same, they both had their jobs to do — and in a matter of days she would return home, never to see him again.

7

Maria was getting into the habit of calling at the barn for a few minutes in the course of the morning. It was allegedly to see how the work was coming along but, in fact, Claire soon realised it was just a chance for a bit of a gossip.

Claire was growing very fond of the older woman. She was blunt and straightforward, but Claire liked that. There was no point in pussyfooting around and being insincere; usually that led to either lying long-term, or being forced to do an about-turn — and that was something that meant trouble when others found out you'd been deceitful.

Maria had a quantity of beans in a bag, a bowl, and a bucket for the shellings. She made herself comfortable on a chair and began to shell the beans. Glancing at Claire's activities now and then, she said pointedly, 'It's a funny profession for a woman.'

Claire laughed softly. 'Do you think so? Plenty of women have moved into areas that used to be male domains these days, Maria. Women drive trains, fly aeroplanes, run building companies, sail ocean liners, drive giant trucks; they're designers, architects, stockbrokers, gardeners, and farmers. The physical work that kept women out of lots of professions is done by machinery these days, so the impossible has become possible. In areas like mine, it has always demanded lots of skill and patience. Women are very good at both of those things.'

Maria added a cackle of agreement and Claire went on, 'Today's world has liberated women and made men step back and think. I often think it's been as much of a revolution for the men as it has been for us.'

'And does that mean you don't want to marry and have children? Are you married to your work?' Her bronzed forehead creased more deeply.

'No. I love my work but I know that it's not everything. I have to earn a living, and I'm enjoying myself, but if I met the right man, I'd try to combine things as best I could. I like children, I'd like my own some day, but I leave that to fate.' She shrugged. 'Meeting someone you want to be with for the rest of your life is a chancey undertaking these days.'

Maria tossed her head, and a handful of beans joined those already in the big white bowl. 'Especially if you are a woman who is as independent minded, stubborn and self-confident as you are,' she said wryly.

Claire went on with her sanding. 'Perhaps, but I don't intend to throw away years of training. Even if I didn't have any restoring work to do, I'd still want to use my time constructively. I enjoy working with my hands.'

She straightened up and surveyed the surface of the wooden block she was shaping.

'What about you — have you never wanted to do anything else? Have you always been here on the farm?'

'I think I told you that I came here as a very young girl to be a housemaid. Those were the days when all the big houses had lots of workers and servants.' Claire nodded and Maria went on, 'It was also a bad time. The Civil War had ended and Franco was in control. Eduardo's grandfather was still young and the family was well known for opposing the Nationalists. He met Eduardo's grandmother while attending a wedding of some relations in London.

'It was very romantic — love at first sight, and it wasn't long before he brought her back to the farm. She was very young and beautiful. When he took over the farm from his father, the officials hereabouts were still rooted in the past and determined to make life as difficult as they could for the family. Today, as then, money was always the main problem on any farm and the family hushed up any amounts of unused money or anything of value, otherwise there'd be unexpected investigations and false accusations.'

Maria took a sip of her coffee before continuing her story.

'There were house searches and all the rest. I remember Eduardo's grandmother telling me she had to hide her jewellery to save it, and I'll never forget how she stood determinedly in front of some of the so-called officials when they turned up one day and threatened to take her furniture away to pay for some family debts they'd invented.

'She warned them that she would go immediately to Madrid with the next train to inform the British government of their treatment of a British citizen. The furniture was her property, she could prove it, and it had nothing to do with the Noriega family. It was a big bluff, of course, I doubt if there would have been a diplomatic crisis over a few pieces of wood. The local officials believed her, though, and crept off with their tails between their legs. They never tried that again.

'Gradually lots of valuable things from the house had to be sold off whenever the farm was going through a bad patch.' She shifted uneasily on the chair and stared out to the sun-filled yard outside. 'Señor Noriega made furtive trips somewhere to sell them. I don't know where he went, no one did, but we are quite near to the French border and it was probably easier for him to follow unguarded routes across the frontier to sell something there than to go somewhere else in Spain where people asked too many questions.'

Claire was quiet for a moment, then murmured, 'It sounds like a very bad time for everyone.'

'It was,' Maria agreed sadly. 'We were all glad when things got back to normal, even if it did take until Franco's death in the seventies. Only then did Señor Noriega feel safe and secure again. You can imagine how we celebrated that night.'

'I bet.' Claire was doing a quick

calculation in her head; if Maria had been a young girl at the end of the Civil War, that meant she was probably into her eighties now. She looked remarkably fit and no one would guess her age at a glance. 'And then you stayed on the farm?'

Maria nodded. 'Eduardo's grandfather died of a heart attack suddenly in 1978, his father died seven years ago, and then Eduardo was left with the farm. He had more or less come to terms with the fact that it would become his responsibility, because his sister had already moved out and married, but I think he hoped that he could have a few years to enjoy trying other things out first, before he came back here for good.'

Claire looked across at Maria. 'I don't think that Eduardo minds. He's trying to make the best out of it and he doesn't seem to hate farming. I have the feeling he loves the horse-breeding side of the business, at least. If all his other ideas work out and make a profit, one day he may be able to employ more help, and enjoy his personal life a lot more.'

Maria nodded. The china bowl was full of beans and the bucket was half-full of shells. She got up and brushed the front of her apron. 'I'd better get back to start getting things ready before the children arrive.' She paused suddenly. 'Oh, heavens! I've run out of salt. I meant to bring some with the last shopping order. I remembered everything else. I was going to ask Eduardo to bring me a packet on his way back from dropping the kids off at school. Ah well, there's nothing for it. I'll just have to walk down to the village to get some.'

Claire gave her an easy smile. 'I'll drive you there. I'll wait for you outside though, because I'd have to change my jeans if I came inside, these are pretty dirty.' She put the block of wood down and slapped the dust off her hands.

'Are you sure it isn't too much trouble?'

'No, of course not. We'll be there and back in ten minutes. Put your beans in the kitchen and I'll meet you outside the door in five minutes. I'll just go to the cottage and brush my hair; it's full of dust.'

Maria gave her a toothy smile and picked up her things. 'Five minutes outside the kitchen.'

* * *

That evening Claire felt confident enough to ask Eduardo, 'What have you done today?'

'Repaired some fences,' he replied easily. 'The whole boundary fence needs to be replaced, but we're taking it a bit at a time, partly because it's hard work, but also because I want to use lasting materials and that makes it an expensive undertaking. I need to spread out the costs so I figure we'll be round everything in a couple of years, but once it's finished it should last my lifetime — I hope, longer than that.'

She filled her fork and asked, 'And you can't use machinery to do it?'

He shook his head. 'Not where it's hilly. Hiring a digger to make the holes might work on level ground, but it's complicated on steep slopes. We have an auger-type hole-digger, a post-rammer, and our muscles. Our method is slower but it works.'

'And as a side-effect, you don't need to go to the gym once you've done that for a couple of hours.'

His even white teeth flashed. 'You're right there.'

'I'm beginning to know where I am when I go for a walk. Is it safe to walk across the fields with the cattle? I don't want to take a chance.'

He laughed. 'Of course you can. They are probably more scared of you than the other way round. Keep to the edge, then if you get too nervous, you can always fly over the hedge.'

'Very reassuring! If I'd known that, I would have bought a broomstick.'

She was hungry and, evidently,

Eduardo was too. They all did justice to Maria's efforts and the conversation flowed easily.

After supplying them all with coffee, Maria said, 'There's a good film on TV this evening. Why don't you stay and watch it with us, Claire?'

Claire hesitated and was startled when Eduardo filled the break in the conversation. 'I'm going out with some friends to a local bar; would you like to come with me instead? You're too young to be stuck in front of the television all the time. Come and see how the Spanish enjoy life.'

Claire was breathless for a second; it was so unexpected and the prospect was spine-tingling. It was probably quite an innocent invitation, but she didn't hesitate. 'Yes — I'd like that, if you're sure I won't get in the way. I hope you haven't forgotten that I can't speak a word of Spanish.'

His eyes twinkled when he said, 'That's not quite true, is it? You can say thank you, please, sorry, cheers, good morning, and good night. Everyone understands a lot of English these days and most people can speak enough, so that I'm sure you'll feel quite comfortable.'

'Do I have to change?'

He grinned. 'Why do women always think they're not wearing the right thing? No, of course not, you look fine. A jacket of some kind would be sensible though — the air cools down quickly in the evening.'

Claire hadn't noticed the surprised expressions that had passed between Maria and Mrs Noriega.

'I'll get my jacket, then. When do you want to leave?'

Eduardo was on his feet too. 'In five minutes?'

Claire repeated. 'Five minutes, okay.'

* * *

As far as Claire was concerned, the evening was a great success. His friends were a friendly bunch of people and open-hearted. They immediately drew her into the centre of things once he'd introduced her, and they plied her with questions about herself and kept her wine glass filled. They were loud and fairly boisterous. Eduardo was more serious than most of them, but everyone clearly liked him.

Claire had no intention of spoiling his evening by monopolising him. He worked hard and deserved to enjoy himself when he got away from the farm. She was pleased and grateful that he'd invited her, but she didn't intend him to feel that he had to entertain her.

There was dance music playing, and whenever she felt Eduardo was watching her too closely, she joined the handful of people on the small dance floor. Generally, one of his friends followed her. Claire wasn't a great disco fan, but dancing was a way to work off extra nervous energy and to have fun with people she liked. She was surprised when Eduardo grabbed her hand and his dark eyes were fathomless as he led her onto the small dance floor.

The music was slow and dreamy, and Claire was content to follow his lead and lean against his muscled body. She didn't dare to look up at his face, in case he noticed how his nearness was affecting her. The wine and the atmosphere were going to her head, and being in his arms for more than a snatched moment was profoundly exhilarating.

She couldn't make up her mind if she was relieved or sorry when the music ended. Eduardo kept hold of her hand and pulled her gently back to the others at the table. She didn't understand what Eduardo answered when someone commented on their reappearance, but they all hooted and laughed.

'What did you say?'

He looked down at her and said fondly, 'I'll tell you another time. What do you want to drink?'

'Nothing, I've had enough alcohol for one evening. Some water would be lovely; I'm thirsty.'

He spoke to the barman and handed her a glass of mineral water. Claire was glad he wasn't someone who tried to push a girl into drinking something she didn't really want. Most of his friends chatted to her in English, and even if they had to search for vocabulary now and then, it was remarkable how well they managed. Claire felt quite ashamed that she could speak so little Spanish.

The enjoyment went on for a while, but it was mid-week and most people had work the following day. Eventually they began to disperse.

Eduardo asked, 'Would you like to hang on a bit longer, or are you ready to go?'

'I'm ready whenever you are. I enjoyed it very much, but everything has to end, and work calls tomorrow.'

He nodded. 'Come on, then.' He slipped his hand through her arm and, after a few sentences to the remaining crowd, they said their goodbyes, and made their way back to his car.

'I like your friends. Thanks for taking

me along tonight.'

'I'm glad you like them. I've known most of them all my life.'

They drove off into the night and as they left the small town, the roads were almost empty. She thought how comfortable and safe she felt with Eduardo.

The shadows wandered and meandered, casting his silhouette in new angles and shapes as they went along. Music played softly and Claire felt contentedly tired.

She was surprised how quickly they reached the turn-off to the farm. He parked the car neatly alongside the house and by the time he came around to her side of the car, Claire was already standing, facing him.

His face was painted in angular shadows.

She smiled up at him and said lightly, 'I'm sure I'll sleep like a log tonight.'

There was silence for a moment, as he stood unmoving in the darkness. 'So will I.'

Claire wasn't sure if she was hoping

for another ending to the evening, but she didn't want to indicate she expected anything more from him, so she kissed his cheek, turned away quickly and went towards the cottage. She didn't look back; if she had, she would have seen that Eduardo was still standing watching her.

* * *

Back at work on the chest of drawers in the barn next morning, Claire glued the supporting blocks to the skirting and left them to dry. One of the bracket feet was badly damaged and, after closer inspection, Claire decided to replace it. She made a cardboard template of one of the other brackets.

It was detailed and time-consuming work, and once she had finally glued everything into place, she had to leave it all to dry for at least twelve hours. Tomorrow she would be able to veneer the rest of the chest. But for now, when she stepped back and viewed the result of her work, she was satisfied.

Claire felt contented. Sometimes in the late afternoon, she went for a walk through the surrounding fields, and even further afield. Now and then she went with one of the children; sometimes on her own. She found her way back easily, now that she had her bearings. She liked the countryside, and she and Eduardo were relaxed together; friends.

She didn't see a lot of him, he was always busy, but when she did, his slow smile brightened the moment and he had a subtly positive effect on her well-being. They faced each other across the dining table each evening and she made an effort not to study him too carefully or pay him too much attention, and the atmosphere remained relaxed.

* * *

The work on the furniture progressed. She'd soon be able to concentrate on the damaged wardrobe — the last item on the list to be repaired.

Claire admitted that she felt pangs of jealousy whenever she saw Elena, galloping on the hills astride a beautiful chestnut horse or visiting the farm. Elena sometimes rode — without greeting her — past the barn, heading towards the stables if she thought Eduardo was there. If he wasn't, she went to the house to find out where he was working.

Claire tried not to take too much notice of the comings and goings, but if Elena was visiting, Claire knew there was only one reason — it had something to do with Eduardo. She hadn't seen Juan since the day he'd suggested she took a short cut to the DIY store and she didn't miss him.

8

One evening after the day's work, it seemed unusually quiet when Claire went across to the main house for the evening meal. She found that she and Maria were alone. 'Where is everyone?'

Maria looked up and began to arrange the dishes for their meal. 'You wouldn't know, but it is Elena's birthday today. She's thirty. Mrs Noriega and Eduardo are honoured guests, so we're on our own.'

Claire felt disappointed. She told herself it was because the cosy evening get-together had been disturbed, but she knew that the real reason was that Eduardo wasn't here, and that he was spending his time with Elena. The thought made her realise how involved with him and his life she'd become. Perhaps it was a good thing that she'd be going home again in a week's time.

Her time in Spain would most likely fade to a pleasant memory, although she'd never forget Eduardo and the others.

Claire sat down and as they ate, the two women were soon chatting about the day's happenings. The room seemed larger with more shadows, and the sound of their voices echoed as they ate their food.

Maria added some more information about Elena's birthday party. 'I expect she is anticipating a special gift from Eduardo.'

Fork poised in mid-air, Claire commented casually, 'And will she get one, do you think?'

Maria shrugged. 'Who can tell what Eduardo will do, or not? If she's expecting something like a ring, I think she'll be disappointed. Somehow, I think I would have noticed Eduardo had something special in mind, if that's where the wind was blowing from.'

'But they're lifelong friends. That counts for an awful lot, doesn't it?'

'Loyalty does, too. I told you once about how she dumped him for better prospects. Eduardo is not likely to forget that.' She laughed dryly. 'Elena is probably beginning to get nervous; thirty years old and not a sign of an engagement ring on the horizon. As far as I know, there's not even another prospect of a serious boyfriend locally.'

'Does she work?'

'She went to university, but I don't think she's ever thought about getting a job. Her father works like a demon on their farm, but neither Elena nor Juan do much to share the burden. I sometimes wonder what will happen when the time comes when he can't manage any more.'

'Perhaps they do more than you think. Even handling the office work is something that no one notices, but it takes up a lot of time.'

Maria shrugged. 'Who knows, but I don't believe either of them think about the fact that everyone has to work for their living in one way or another.

Those two have been spoiled all their lives, and it's too late now for their father to turn the wheel around and bring them into line. Their mother died a couple of years ago and that's made the situation even worse. Juan will end up a wild one if they don't curb him soon.'

The conversation then drifted to Pablo and his wife, as well as other topics.

Maria suddenly interposed, 'I wonder why they didn't invite you to the party? I know you're only here for a while, but Spanish people are usually very hospitable and you do know Elena.'

'I was asking myself why she didn't invite you.'

Maria's eyes twinkled. 'Because I'm a servant, of course. Elena pretends to be open-minded but she believes everyone should keep to their place in life, and mine is in the kitchen.'

Claire was annoyed. 'How ridiculous! You've known her all her life.'

'She chooses to forget people that

she's known all her life when she wants her house full of rich and beautiful people. Apparently, a couple of her school friends from the village are up in arms because they weren't invited either.'

When they'd finished the meal and Claire had praised it, Maria made an exception and allowed Claire to help with the washing-up. Shaking out the teacloth, Claire suddenly had an idea. 'Why don't you come across to the cottage for an hour instead of watching TV? It's such a lovely evening. We can sit out at the front and have a chat. You could bring your knitting. I have a bottle of wine I bought last time I went through the village. I'm no judge of whether it is a good wine or not, but a glass or two won't harm either of us, will it?'

Maria hesitated a second and then nodded, smiling. Claire felt pleased. Somehow, she felt that Maria was feeling disillusioned because she'd been ignored, and if that was the case, she was glad she could provide her with a little diversion.

Maria fetched her knitting from a nearby cupboard and they went across the yard to make themselves comfortable in some cushioned chairs outside Claire's doorway. Claire put Maria's glass of wine within her reach on a nearby window ledge. She was content to put hers to the side of her chair on the ground.

Maria began to knit and the clicking of the needles merged with the sound of the crickets and other insects of the night nearby. Claire didn't ask what the knitting was going to be, and Maria gave her no information. The half-finished creation rested on her lap like a swirling ocean of greys and blues.

Claire asked, 'Did you never want to marry, Maria?'

Maria went on knitting. 'Why do you suppose that anyone would want to marry someone like me? But there was a chap, when I was young and pretty. He was a sailor; came from the village, but the sea was in his blood. He promised me he would settle down one day, but he never did.'

'A sailor? Did he have a girl in every port?'

'No, I don't think so. You never know, of course, but I think he just wanted to see the world. Perhaps he would have settled down here in the village eventually, or somewhere nearby in the end — who knows?'

'What happened?'

'He picked up some disease or other in Panama. There were only days between him falling ill and the morning he died. I know his sister very well, and she told me. Most people didn't know that he and I were going out together.

'I think he liked me because I never tried to force him to change his lifestyle and stay on land. I knew how he needed to spread his wings; I just hoped that one day he'd have enough of all the roaming and would want to settle down with a wife and start a family.'

'How sad. What was he like?'

The needles ceased their clicking. 'He was a good-looking man; tall, dark, with eyes full of fire. He could eat like a horse. No one ever pushed him around, and people liked him . . . and he loved children.'

Claire was silent for a moment. 'He sounds like someone very special.'

'He was . . . ' The older woman was gazing, unseeing, into the far off dusk.

'And you never wanted another friend after that?'

'Oh, now and then the idea crossed my mind, but times weren't good and so many men were involved in the Civil War in those days. You never knew if they'd sneak off in the middle of the night and be killed. If I did ever meet anyone I liked, I usually ended up making comparisons to Paulo, and that never worked.'

She shifted in her seat and the needles started moving once again. 'It was just one of those things — fate or whatever you choose to call it. I've still managed to have a good life here. This family is my family, and the Noriegas have always treated me as one of their own.'

There was silence for a few moments, and then Maria continued. 'Paulo told me the most wonderful stories whenever he came back. About headhunters in Borneo, about Australia, India, and Africa. He went all over the world and brought back amazing tales.

'I still don't know whether they were always true or whether he was just trying to play tricks on me.

'I remember one story in particular. He told me they were somewhere in South America, and they'd been persuaded by a missionary to take some goods up the river to some primitive tribe living in the jungle. When they got to this village, the people were practically naked and painted themselves in red and blue because they thought that looked so fine. He also said the younger men had kinds of weights on their private parts because it was considered very manly to have long ones.'

Claire spluttered and brushed some wine from her lips. 'What?' She gave a peal of laughter and it echoed across the yard. 'Maria! That can't be true, can it?'

Their combined laughter filled the night as two figures emerged unexpectedly out of the shadows — Eduardo and his farming neighbour, Philip De Silva. Approaching them, Eduardo asked, 'What's so funny?'

Their laughter had been slowly subsiding; but when Maria and Claire looked up at the two men, they simultaneously rocked with laughter again. Claire brushed the laughter tears away from the corner of her eyes and tried to compose herself long enough to reply.

'Don't ask us to explain. Something you wouldn't understand, and even if we tried, I don't think you would think it was very funny either.'

Looking slightly irritated, Eduardo stood in the shadows watching them. 'At the moment you seem to be having more fun here than we're having back there.' He moved closer.

Claire tried to sound sensible. 'We're enjoying ourselves — aren't we, Maria?' Maria nodded vigorously. 'Don't worry about us, go ahead and have fun, we're doing fine here.'

'Philip presumed you two were invited and, when I said you hadn't received any kind of invitation, he insisted on coming to fetch you personally,' Eduardo told them.

Philip looked at them appraisingly. 'If you don't come across, is there a chance of us getting a glass of wine here?'

Claire lifted the bottle and squinted at the contents. 'Not really. We've almost finished this one. Perhaps Maria can pinch one from the house?'

Eduardo rolled a nearby barrel on its rim towards them, and used it to sit down.

He said, 'I won't allow that, so you'll just have to get your skates on, and come back to the party with us.'

Maria looked as if she was about to protest again, but Philip threw his arm around her shoulder and launched into rapid and persuasive Spanish.

Eduardo obliged, by translating the conversation for Claire. 'He just said, 'Come on, Maria, take no notice of Elena, you know what she's like. Sometimes I think my daughter has lost touch with reality. Go and put your party frock on.' He wants you to come, too, Claire.'

Both Maria and Claire were still reluctant, because they weren't Elena's guests, but Philip De Silva was insistent and clearly wouldn't be deterred, so they finally allowed themselves be persuaded. Philip declared he wouldn't go back without Maria, and Eduardo insisted Claire couldn't stay on her own.

Eduardo said in a low voice, 'I don't like parties where what you own is obviously more important than who you are — so if you don't come back with us, I won't go back either.'

Maria and Claire looked at each other and Maria shrugged. 'Anything for a quiet life!'

The two men were pleased. Philip said, 'We give you ten minutes to change, if you want to.'

Eduardo said, 'I'll go and ask Pablo's wife to sit with the children for a couple of hours.'

Maria scuttled off across the yard, and Claire dashed upstairs to change into the only dress she'd brought with her. It had a white background and poppies dotted here and there. A quick renewal of lipstick and a brush through her auburn locks was all she had time for, but she thought she could see approval in Eduardo's eyes when she rejoined them.

A minute or so later Maria joined them in a pale grey silk dress with touches of lace at the collar and cuffs. Claire thought she looked impressive, and told her so.

When they reached the De Silva home, Claire found it was similar in design to the Noriega's.

She didn't get much of a chance to see the inside because the party was being held outside under the stars, on a huge patio at the back of the house.

Elena greeted them with apprehension on her face. Maria simply shook hands and didn't congratulate her. Elena knew that Maria had been hurt and wouldn't forget. Once the awkward part was over, though, they could enjoy themselves, and Claire did.

She met lots of other neighbours from the immediate vicinity, and Eduardo was her shadow; he introduced her, translated for her and acted as her guardian. Eventually, they bumped into Juan in the throng of people. He had a young woman at his side, and she was clearly under his spell. He spotted them before they reached him; no one could overlook Eduardo's tall figure, even in a crowd this size.

Juan nodded leisurely. 'Ah, the English rose. How's life?'

Claire met his glance and although she was angry because she knew he'd definitely given her the directions down the side-road to the DIY without any kind of warning, she didn't want to spoil the party.

'I'm fine, thanks, and you?'

Eduardo didn't intend to leave without baiting him, however and the animosity between the two men was tangible as Eduardo almost growled, 'And that's no thanks to you . . . '

Juan took an unhurried sip from his glass and answered with a casual, 'And what does that mean?'

Claire heard how Eduardo's voice was increasing in irritation. 'You know exactly what I mean. I don't know why you did it but I'm warning you to never to try such a stupid trick like that again. Claire could easily have been killed.'

With a thin-lipped smile, Juan drawled, 'Eduardo, you have a strong tendency to dream up things that are not true. You ought to be careful; you'll get yourself into real trouble, accusing people wrongly.'

'You're the one who's up to his neck in trouble. There are plenty of rumours about you and your behaviour making the rounds. Only someone who is sick in the head could play a joke like that. Grow up, Juan! If you would only remember that the world was not made just to revolve around you. Everything will spin completely out of control for you one day. Think of your family at least.'

The two men stared stonily at each other.

Juan looked pale under his tan. 'If I want advice, I'll ask for it, otherwise mind your own business!' he snarled. 'I repeat that I don't know what you're talking about. I only gave Claire directions for a short cut. If she misunderstood me, I'm not to blame. It's regrettable of course, but these things happen.'

Claire just wanted to get away. She placed her hand on Eduardo's arm.

'Eduardo, leave it. I'd like something to drink — and I haven't said hello to your mother yet, either.'

Throwing a cold glance in Juan's direction, Eduardo nodded and took Claire's elbow; she could feel the hardness and tension in the muscles of his arm as they turned away.

Juan called after them, 'Anyway why are you so bothered? You won in the end, didn't you?'

* * *

The rest of the evening was good. They avoided Juan, or he avoided them, Claire wasn't sure which was the case. Everyone was friendly and welcoming and the memory of dancing with Eduardo under a star-sprinkled sky would live with her forever.

Later, more of the women joined in when the flamenco music began. Young and old, they were all immediately attracted by the sound. Claire was delighted to notice Maria among them, making graceful movements with her arms and feet. The rhythm of the music was fascinating and with Eduardo at her side, she felt life couldn't offer anything better.

They met Maria later among a group of her cronies. Eduardo handed her a glass of wine and Maria asked casually, 'Did you give Elena a present?'

'Of course I did, you don't go to a birthday party without bringing a present.'

'We did — she didn't deserve anything,' Maria said sharply. 'What did you give her?'

'You are sometimes much too curious and it's really none of your business, Maria. But if you must know, I bought her a bottle of perfume — her favourite perfume. Moreover, before you ask how I knew, she's been telling me what her favourite perfume is for the last ten years in the hope that I'd buy her some one day. Women are like that.'

'Was she happy with it?'

'I think so; I expect so. Why shouldn't she be?'

'Oh, no special reason,' Maria said with a wry smile.

Moving on, Maria introduced Claire to someone from the village and translated for her, Maria adding with obvious pride, 'My acquaintances in the village are in awe of me because I speak English; most of my friends know only a word or two.'

Claire said, 'The fact that you speak English at all is wonderful. It meant I didn't have to make the slightest effort, or even walk around with a dictionary in my hand.'

Eduardo laughed, then finished his glass of wine in one gulp and looked at his watch. 'I'd better find my mother; she was talking to a bunch of acquaintances whom she hasn't seen for a while. I have a business meeting tomorrow morning.'

Claire said, 'I'll come with you — otherwise you'll just have to look for me as well later.'

Eduardo replied quickly, 'No, wait here, I'll come back for you. Are you coming with us, Maria?'

Maria lifted her glass. 'Marina and I have a lot to talk about. Carry on. Someone else will give me a lift home.'

They both watched him disappear among the throng. Maria remarked, 'He's a good lad. His heart's in the right place. One in a million.'

Claire was in absolute agreement — but she couldn't say so.

* * *

Another day passed and the chest of drawers was finally finished. Everyone was full of praise for the results and Claire was hard at work on the three-piece desk suite — a water-stained writing table, a couple of pigeon-hole shelves and a wall-mounted cabinet. It looked sorry for itself and Claire wondered whether it had been left outside in the rain and no one had thought to dry it off later.

Claire could tell the desk wasn't English in origin; in all probability, it was a French piece from the end of the nineteenth century. She didn't intend to tell the family that.

They believed all the furniture was entirely English and there was no reason to spoil their illusions. They didn't intend to sell any of it, and it had nothing to do with her restoration work.

She began by cleaning, stripping, and strengthening the joints. Once the pieces had been dismantled and cleaned, they were re-glued, and everything reassembled.

Alisa spent one dismal afternoon in the barn playing with Antonio's Nintendo and chatting. Claire asked her if she was any happier about riding nowadays.

Alisa beamed. 'Yes, it's a lot more fun now. I'm on my own and Uncle Eduardo doesn't mind that I'm practising on Josepha. Josepha is such a lovely, gentle horse. I love her.'

'That's good. You're enjoying it now, then?'

'Yes. I'm so glad I told Uncle Eduardo how I was feeling.'

'So am I. I hope that you'll like it more and more, as time goes on. One day, you'll manage bigger horses, but there's no rush, I'm sure.'

Alisa nodded in agreement. 'Uncle Eduardo told me that too, and he's going to explain everything to Mum and Dad.'

* * *

Claire attacked the peeling veneer on the writing-table section. The days flew by, and although she was completely focused on finishing the work, she looked forward with increasing pleasure to the evening meal. She told herself it was because of the family atmosphere, but deep down she knew it was because she could see Eduardo for a while. He still came to look at her work from time and time, and Claire couldn't stop her pulse racing whenever she saw him.

It was stupid, because she knew that

their contact would be ending soon. She had no reason to believe he'd miss her when she went; perhaps he'd even be glad to see her go. He was always polite and helpful, but ever since that day they'd gone for a walk to his grandmother's cottage there had been something reserved about him. Probably no one got really close to him, or knew what he was thinking. He was in control of his life, and obviously wanted to keep it that way.

Elena called at the farmhouse; presumably, she wanted to meet Eduardo. Claire was sitting outside the barn in the morning sun drinking coffee, and Elena gave her the briefest of glances as she passed, barely nodding at her.

Claire called politely, 'Morning, Elena.'

Elena left a waft of perfume in her wake. It was very exotic and strong; not Claire's kind of perfume at all. Probably it was Eduardo's birthday gift. Apparently, Eduardo was not where she expected to find him at the stables, because Elena returned a few minutes later slapping her whip in her hand as she went back to her horse.

She climbed into the saddle like a tournament competitor and tore off into the distance without a word.

That afternoon, Eduardo called by and asked if she needed anything from the DIY store again. Claire grabbed the chance. She did actually need some glue, but she could have fetched that herself at any time. No, she used the excuse of going along with him because she said she needed him to read the label to know if the contents were suitable for antique furniture, or not. But the truth was that Claire was just glad of a chance to be on her own with him.

She hadn't worked out why he attracted her like no one she'd ever met before. Was it because he was Spanish and all the romantic stories about Hispanic grandees had emerged from her subconscious, or was it simply just a physical attraction?

She tried to avoid the thought that perhaps it was something stronger . . .

As she expected, she enjoyed the trip. He left her outside the store entrance and went off to pick up some agricultural bits and pieces from another nearby retailer. When she emerged from the store she waited for him, holding more than she'd intended to buy. On his return he eyed her arms full of purchases and gave her a lop-sided, knowing smile.

Once she was sitting in the passenger seat, he didn't ask, he simply drove to the café they'd visited after their first shopping excursion together. His friend's mother was just as friendly, the cake and the coffee were just as good. The conversation between them flowed unhindered.

She felt bubbly and wholly alive in his presence, and as they talked, she decided she enjoyed being with him more and more. They were in accord about most things and it was easy to share serious discussions or light-hearted moments with him. It was pleasantly warm in the sun, but the café's roadside tables were in the shade, and an occasional breeze cooled her flushed cheeks. She couldn't guess what he was feeling but his dark eyes sparkled as he watched her. His rangy body was relaxed and he smiled at her across the checked tablecloth in a way that sent her senses into turmoil.

On their way back, they passed Elena close to the farm in her Mini. Eduardo sounded the horn and her smile faded instantly when she spotted Claire alongside him. But she recovered quickly and waved back.

Claire wondered why the arrogant woman acted as she did. She had all the time in the world to win Eduardo, if that was what she wanted.

Claire didn't like the idea of Eduardo and Elena together; she felt he deserved someone nicer. And there was a hard knot in her stomach whenever she thought about Eduardo with a wife . . . any wife.

She stored away the memories and the conversations and realised she was falling hopelessly into a bottomless pit of love for Eduardo Noriega.

9

Maria came around to the cottage the next morning with a piece of cake and a toothy smile. Claire couldn't be disgruntled with her, even though she was dying to get on with the veneering.

Claire munched on the light-as-a-feather sponge and resolved to try to gather more information about the family.

'When I went for a walk with Eduardo and the children a little while ago we went to his gran's cottage,' she remarked. 'I've been wondering what would have happened when Eduardo's grandmother lived there if a fire broke out. If she couldn't get to the door, she wouldn't have been able to climb through the windows because of the bars.'

Maria wiped her hands on her apron. 'I don't think she ever thought about that sort of thing. The bars were only put in place after Señora Noriega died, and I think it was only done then to make the place safe from would-be burglars.'

Claire nodded. 'It's very isolated, isn't it? I'm surprised his gran wanted to live so far away from the main house, especially when the farmhouse is beautiful and comfortable. Why did she need the cottage?'

Maria shrugged and said, 'She enjoyed being on her own; she read a lot.'

'She wanted her own special place, I suppose.' Claire began polishing again and Maria looked on with interest.

'I can't imagine anyone wanting to live there now,' Maria added. 'It will cost a lot of money to do it up; not worth Eduardo bothering. He needs his money for more important things.' She nodded in the direction of Claire's work. 'It's coming along fine. When that's finished there's only the wardrobe?'

Claire refolded her cloth and looked up. 'Yes. I don't know how much work that will need yet, but I'll find out soon enough.'

* * *

Later that evening they were together again, enjoying the evening meal. If Eduardo's glance rested more often than usual on Claire, no one seemed to notice.

She was enjoying her dessert when Sophia Noriega surprised her. 'I'm going in to Santander tomorrow. Maria is coming; would you like come, too, Claire?'

Claire was taken aback but she liked the idea; she hadn't had much chance to play the tourist since she arrived, and it would be nice to see something else of the area before she left.

Mrs Noriega continued, 'I don't go to town very often, but now and then we have to stock up on things that are easier to find in a bigger place like

Santander. Maria enjoys the bustle, don't you, Maria? But by the end of the day, we are reminded exactly why we like living here on the farm, and not in the town.'

Claire answered, 'I think I'd enjoy that, actually. Thanks for asking me.'

'If you only want to go on a shopping spree, you can come with us; we're going to Maliano because there are some good shopping malls there, but if you'd rather look around the town, we can leave you near the cathedral and we'll all meet up for coffee in the afternoon.

'The old part of the town was burned down, so there isn't so much for a tourist to see any more, but there are still a couple of interesting buildings.'

Claire nodded. 'That sounds perfect. I'd prefer to look around the cathedral and take in the atmosphere there for a while.'

She decided to follow them into the living room with its long terrace looking out towards the mountains far off to the north. Eduardo joined them for a while and Claire had to stop herself looking unnecessarily in his direction. He sat in one of the comfortable armchairs with a newspaper and a glass of wine on a nearby side-table. But before long, he left them with a general goodnight to everyone. She heard him going through the kitchen and guessed he was going to the stables to check on his beloved horses before he went to bed.

* * *

Next day was fine and dry; the temperatures reminded her of good English summer days. They met up after breakfast and Claire offered to drive, but Señora Noriega brushed her offer aside. 'I'm used to the traffic and know where to park. Another time, perhaps?'

Claire didn't think there would be another time, but she didn't say so.

It was a pleasant journey and Claire looked at the scenery along the route with interest. The two older women left her near the Cathedral and she strolled around. She found that, as Mrs Noriega had forewarned, there wasn't much of an 'old' centre, but there were exclusive boutiques and expensive antique shops leading off the main square. Claire enjoyed rummaging around, though she didn't buy anything apart from a couple of postcards and something to drink.

Strolling along the edge of the main square she was startled to hear someone call her name. Looking around, she saw Elena De Silva. Claire masked her frown of exasperation; she'd planned to enjoy the freedom of an afternoon alone, and she didn't need someone like Elena.

Elena was dressed in a figure-hugging fashionable two-piece. Her make-up was more obvious than usual and her black hair was formed into a perfect, smart chignon. She looked like a model from a glossy magazine. Claire smoothed her own trousers and jacket into place, and was glad that, for once, she felt smart. It was the only stylish outfit she'd brought with her, even if it was on the casual side of smart.

'What are you doing here? Shopping?' Elena asked brightly.

'No. I came with Mrs Noriega and Maria. They're shopping and will pick me up later. I'm looking at the tourist attractions.' Claire waited.

Elena nodded in the direction of the various boutiques with their exclusive window displays. 'It's a very expensive part of town here, but you can find some wonderful things if you know where to look, and search long enough.'

Claire held her glance. 'Visiting boutiques have never been top priority on my list of things to do.'

Elena looked at her closely, running a well-practised eye over Claire's clothes. 'Yes, I can tell that, but I suppose everyone decides what's personally important or not.'

Her answer was rude but Claire gave her the benefit of the doubt and answered, 'I've always had to work for a living and never earned enough to afford designer clothes. I think that even if I did, I'd be reluctant to spend my money on things that are highly fashionable one day and out of fashion the next. You can buy nice clothes without bankrupting yourself.'

Elena's laugh tinkled. 'Perhaps, but men like Eduardo expect their women to look first-class. Second-best just won't do.'

Claire shrugged. 'Are you sure about that? Clearly, you think clothes are more important than I do. To be honest, I can't imagine that Spanish men are so different to any others. They choose their girlfriends for more than just clothes sense.'

Slightly irritated, Elena's eyebrows lifted. 'You seem to think you know all about Spanish men.'

Claire shook her head. 'No, I'm sure I don't. I just think that any man would be happiest with someone who fits his lifestyle. If he's a bank manager, his wife will need a wardrobe for dinner-parties; if she's married to a farmer, she'll need more practical, working clothes.'

Clearly Elena wasn't smitten by the idea of the duties of a working farmer's wife. Tossing her handbag around nervously, she glanced down at her pale-grey high-heeled shoes and then at her watch. 'I must rush. I'm meeting an old school-friend, and I want to be back in time to go out riding with Eduardo later on. You don't ride, do you? Such a pity. Well, enjoy yourself.'

'Thanks.' Claire knew that Elena didn't care one way or the other whether she enjoyed herself or not.

Claire was glad to be on her own again and wandered along without noticing where she was going.

She was still deep in thought. She hoped Eduardo wouldn't end up with Elena; he didn't deserve someone who wanted only social standing and financial security. She didn't think that Eduardo could afford someone like

Elena either; Señorita Da Silva wasn't someone who wouldn't change her lifestyle without a fight. But Eduardo and Elena had grown up together and, according to Maria, at one time they'd been on course for more than mere friendship.

That could still be possible; Elena certainly seemed to think so. Claire had the feeling Maria didn't approve of Elena, but she'd have to accept her if that was how things ended. Eduardo would always go his own way and make his own choices.

When she met up with the two older women again a short time later, they went to a local café. With an effort, Claire pushed Elena and Eduardo from her mind and simply enjoyed the coffee. In their company, she felt relaxed and stress-free.

When they all arrived back at the farm a short time later, apart from meeting Elena, Claire decided it had been a very good day.

She checked that the latest layer of

veneer was drying successfully and it was soon time to share a makeshift evening meal of various local cheeses, olives and sausage with Maria and Señora Noriega.

Claire could tell they were both tired after their excursions so after the meal, she left them to go back to the cottage.

Eduardo hadn't been there anyway, and she wondered if he was still out riding with Elena — or if he had a date with her somewhere in Santander.

Claire spent a sleepless night that night as she tossed and turned and thought about all that had happened in the last couple of weeks.

She'd arrived free of any ties, and now she loved Eduardo Noriega and always would; she was certain it wasn't some kind of passing infatuation. She was physically attracted and she felt enormous respect for what he was doing for the farm and his family. It showed her what kind of man he was and she admired him, as well as loving him.

He meant more to her than anyone she had ever met. She wanted him to be happy, even if that meant him being happy with someone else — and that showed just how much she loved him, didn't it?

* * *

The three-piece desk piece now had a glorious sheen. When it was in place, she could imagine the pigeon-holes filled with letters and papers, the cabinet filled with ornaments and generally giving an overall impression that was very majestic. The fact that it had a very practical writing table made it even more attractive in her eyes.

She remembered Eduardo's instruction not to try to move anything on her own, so she wandered across to the kitchen, shared a coffee with Maria and asked her to tell Eduardo and Pablo they could move it into the house whenever they had time.

She'd heard they were out making

hay in one of the fields, so she added, 'Don't bother them, though; it doesn't need to be today; they'll be tired after a day in the fields. Today, tomorrow, next week — it doesn't matter; it's safe enough where it is.'

Maria looked at her shrewdly and nodded.

'So, that's all the furniture I had out in the barn. Now there's just the wardrobe. Can I take a look? Eduardo mentioned that one leg is damaged, but otherwise it was in good shape.'

Maria nodded. 'Of course. I need to prepare lunch now, though, so can you come back later this afternoon? After the children are back from school and have had their lunch?'

Claire got up.

'Of course. I think I'll go to the supermarket now. I need a couple of personal things. Can I bring you anything back?'

Maria's brow wrinkled. 'Well, I would like some more dried red beans.'

'No problem, as long as you write

down the exact name and brand you want so that I know exactly what I have to look for.'

Getting up, Maria bustled off to one of the cupboards and emptied the remains of a packet into one of the saucepans. She handed Claire the empty sachet and said, 'Just look for these.'

'Great, that's easy. See you later, then.'

The older woman nodded and watched her walk across the yard. Things were not going so well in that young woman's life any more, Maria thought. She'd lost some of her carefree spontaneity and her eyes didn't sparkle any more.

* * *

Claire browsed around the supermarket, wondering what some of the foodstuff on sale would be like when it was cooked; she enjoyed looking and guessing. Every country had its preferences and partialities. One of the women she'd met when Eduardo took her with him to meet his friends was passing down one of the aisles, and recognised Claire. She stopped to say hello and ask how Eduardo was in perfect English. Claire tried to answer cheerfully and they passed the time of day for a few minutes, but her heart just wasn't in it.

She eventually found Maria's beans and, together with her own purchases, she made her way to the cash desk and managed to pay.

On the way to her Jeep, she came face to face with Juan De Silva. He hadn't come near the farm since Elena's birthday and she could have done without meeting him now, but her polite upbringing meant she didn't want to ignore him. 'Hello, Juan,' she said.

'Hello, English rose! I thought we'd never meet again. What a pleasant surprise.'

His eyes narrowed and Claire didn't like the way he was looking at her. She nodded, impatient to get away.

He smiled, but his eyes were flat and unreadable.

'I saw you out at the old cottage recently,' he said.

'Did you? That's a while back, isn't it?'

'That cottage has become a rendezvous location since Eduardo's grandmother died. There's isn't a better place for miles if you want to meet someone when other people are not supposed to know about it.'

'I thought the cottage was empty and cold, and it's locked,' she countered. 'I can't imagine it would be very comfortable for any kind of meeting.'

He laughed softly. 'Who needs comfort? You only need somewhere to lie down.' He looked at her greedily. 'Have you ever asked Elena or Eduardo if they use it?'

Claire didn't like the insinuation. She wanted to get away. She looked at her watch. 'I must be off, I'm late already. Goodbye, Juan!'

'Perhaps we'll meet again?'

Hurrying away, she called back to him non-committally over her shoulder. 'Perhaps.'

Driving back, she wondered if Juan was just trying to spread scandal by hinting that Eduardo and Elena were lovers and met secretly at the cottage — or whether there was truth behind his insinuations.

When she got back to the farm, she delivered the beans to Maria and promised to play table tennis with the children later that afternoon. She did, and after they had both beaten her several times, she left them gleefully celebrating and went back to the house to look at the wardrobe.

Maria took her up the curved stone staircase and down a long corridor. 'Along here, it is in one of the guest rooms. I think it has always been in here since the Señora brought it from England.' She flung open the door and went ahead to open the curtains and unfasten the latches on the windows.

The large pine double wardrobe was standing along the wall opposite the windows. Claire guessed that it dated from the end of the nineteenth century. It was in good condition and a lovely honey colour, with moulded edges, two large lower drawers and a fitted hanging rail. One of the feet had been pushed out of line at some time in the past, and someone had placed a similar-sized block of wood to support the structure at that point. She knelt and took a closer look.

Getting up again, she said, 'It's a straightforward break; probably the wood was faulty and it just gave way. I'll need to make a new foot, but that's no great problem because I just have to copy the one on the other side. I'd like to have it lying on the floor, though. There is no way I can fit a new foot when it's standing upright. The repair will need time to be joined and glued. Is there much inside?'

Maria opened it and commented, 'I think these are some of Eduardo's grandmother's clothes. I can pile them on the bed in the meantime.'

Claire nodded. 'And I can remove the doors and the drawers, so that it will be easier to handle. Perhaps Eduardo and Pablo can turn it on its back when they're moving the other piece from the barn to the house. It's definitely not worth the bother of transporting it out to the barn. I'll cover the floor and I promise not to make a mess.'

* * *

Next morning Maria came across to the cottage when Claire was still having breakfast. 'The men are moving the furniture,' she told her.

Claire hurried to join them. Her heart lifted when she saw Eduardo and it cost no effort to smile at him.

The men had already transported the lower section of the restored desk into the hall.

Eduardo gave her an encouraging

look. 'Where shall we put it, do you think?'

'Shouldn't you ask your mother?'

'I have, and she couldn't make up her mind. She told me to ask you.'

Claire didn't take long to decide. 'I honestly think it will look great just there, against the wall. It will be an eye-catcher whenever someone enters the hall. Perhaps you'll be able to find a matching chair from that period one day, and complete the picture?'

Eduardo rubbed his chin and considered. 'Yes, I think you're right. Let's put it against the wall, Pablo.'

Claire put up her hand. 'Not right up against it; I still have to join the upper and lower sections securely to make it safe, so I'll need a gap wide enough for me to move behind it. Once I've done that, it can be moved right up against the wall.'

The two men went off to fetch the upper section and, on their return, they carefully mounted it on the lower part. It glowed, almost as if it was delighted to be on display again.

'Can you lower the wardrobe upstairs onto its back on the tarpaulin before you go? I've covered the floor so as not to make a mess — Maria will scalp me if I do — but I need to get at the damaged leg.'

Eduardo considered her; he rested his hands on his hips. 'You're a slave-driver, do you know that?'

'Am I? I don't think so. You're the one who told me not to lift heavy furniture, remember?'

He grinned and shrugged. 'I was only joking. If you join the two desk sections together and, in the meantime, we'll tip the wardrobe onto its back. When we come down, we'll put this against the wall.'

'Thanks,' she replied with a smile.

Several minutes later, they were back again and the men positioned the full desk suite carefully against the wall. Everyone stood back to look.

Eduardo said, 'It's really good work, Claire, and it looks just perfect — as if it has always belonged right there.'

Filled with pride in her own work, she nodded. 'Once it has papers and things in it, it will look even better.'

* * *

It was too late to do much more that afternoon, but Claire removed the damaged foot from the wardrobe, and stencilled a copy of one from the other side.

Back in the barn, she picked out a suitable piece of pinewood and began to carefully transfer the outline.

She sawed away the unnecessary corners and started working on the rest with chisels and sandpaper. By the time she saw it was time to clean up for dinner, she'd already made very good progress.

10

Across the scrubbed table, Claire watched her hosts in the glow of the lamplight and tried to store some of the feeling and memories. She knew that once the wardrobe foot had been replaced, there was no other reason for her to linger.

She jumped when she realised that Eduardo had been talking to her. 'Pardon? Sorry I was miles away.'

He raised his brows and returned dryly, 'That's where I'll be in two days time — miles away.'

Her heart skipped a beat. 'Oh, where are you going?'

'To look at some second-hand farm machinery. Someone is offering something we need, to get our harvesting finished faster. Perhaps I can knock the price down a bit when I meet the farmer.'

She absent-mindedly took some sweet almonds from the dish in the centre. 'It seems that farmers are always bargaining.'

He laughed. 'Yes, I enjoy trying to get something cheaper. Most farmers are shrewd and perceptive. The one I'm going to see has a larger place than this and he's better off.

'He's decided he needs something bigger, so I'm hoping he'll be sympathetic when I explain that we are living on bread-crusts and olives.'

Claire spluttered and put her hand in front of her mouth to prevent an explosion of almonds across the table. 'I thought you always told the truth. I'm beginning to wonder if you'll pay me for my work now.'

He gave an irresistible, devastating grin. 'I will, promise, even if Maria has to feed us on red beans and cheap sausage for the rest of our lives.'

Maria and Señora Noriega joined in the laughter.

Claire loved him so much and she

liked the two older women. She knew she was going to miss them all like crazy when she finally went home.

* * *

Next morning she began early and finished off the new foot by lunchtime. She was satisfied; cut, polished and stained, there was no dissimilarity in the colour or the texture. The foot was a perfect match.

Maria wasn't in the kitchen, and she couldn't find Señora Noriega either, but she felt familiar enough with the family to go on ahead into the house and she took the stone steps at the double, then headed down the corridor to the room where the wardrobe lay. She held the new foot in the right position to see how it looked. It was ideal.

Gathering the necessary tools and some glue, she sat down and made herself comfortable, ready to start the last stage of replacement. Tipping her head to the right and the left, trying to see the exact position where the foot would fit, something at the back suddenly caught her eye.

She'd seen enough antique furniture to notice that there was an unusual four-sided piece of wood running along the back. Going down on her knees and then lying prostrate to reach the back, she ran her fingers along it, and then back again.

She found what she expected and when she pressed the metal pin there was a click and an oblong cavity opened halfway along its length.

Her excitement grew. Anyone loved to find secret compartments, and even if it was her job to work with old furniture, it was still fascinating to find a hiding place. She could see things wrapped in cloth in the cavity.

Standing up, she decided she'd gone far enough on her own. She had to find Eduardo and his mother.

She found him by the stables exercising one of the horses. He came towards her and noticed her heightened colour. 'Is something wrong?'

'No, I don't think so — quite the opposite, in fact. I want you to come with me — I've found something. Where's your mother?'

'She was chatting to Pablo's wife last time I saw her.'

His brow wrinkled with curiosity.

'Fetch her, please, Eduardo, and come up to the bedroom. Oh, and Maria — she should come, too.'

'She's hanging up washing. Whatever's going on, Claire?'

With a bright smile, she said, 'Just fetch the others and come up to the bedroom and I'll show you.'

Ten minutes later, she showed Eduardo the hidden cavity.

'Well, I'll be damned! A secret compartment.'

Claire was almost more excited than the others. 'Go on! Take out whatever's in there . . . what is it?'

Lying on the floor he reached backwards. 'Hang on, give me a chance to reach it first.'

Maria and Mrs Noriega stood waiting impatiently as he held the first bundle in his hand. He untied it and suddenly they all stared in amazement at the jewellery in his hand. It was tightly packed, and clearly valuable. Precious stones sparkled in the sunlight from the nearby window. They all stared, speechless.

Maria broke the silence. 'There they are! We all thought your grandfather had sold everything of value, but then those things were your grandmother's. He hung on to her jewellery after all, despite everything.'

Claire peered into the cavity. 'I think there's more in there.'

Still looking slightly dazed, Eduardo handed the jewellery to his mother and reached into the cavity with his long fingers. He pulled out a roll from the left side, a bundle of yellowed papers, and another roll from the right.

He got up, handed his mother the papers and, unrolling the cloth, he revealed gold coins. Once he tipped them onto the bedcover, they made a very sizeable pile.

They all stared in silence at each other and at the finds for several moments before Maria and Mrs Noriega broke into excited chatter.

Eduardo beamed when he looked at Claire. 'This is fantastic,' he said. 'I can't imagine how much they're worth, but the price of gold is sky-high at the moment.'

Pleased for him and the family, she replied, 'Yes, I read about that in the newspapers not long ago. Perhaps someone professional should advise you about whether it would be better to cash it in straight away, or not. I presume your grandfather hid it in there for safe keeping?'

Mrs Noriega clapped her hands excitedly. 'I knew my father was secretive. Everyone believed we lost all the money after the Civil War; but he was probably just scared to show there was anything left over. I'd completely forgotten that my mother had some valuable jewellery.'

Claire remarked, 'It does explain why your mother made you promise never to let the furniture leave the property, doesn't it? Perhaps if someone lives through a civil war like that, it changes their attitude to money and other valuables.'

Sophia nodded. 'Oh, how exciting! This will make such a difference; for you most of all, Eduardo. You'll be able to do all the things you planned to do in the future — now.'

Eduardo stood with his hands on his hips and regarded them all. 'Yes, you're right there. But let's not get too excited yet; we don't know how much money is involved. And the jewellery is yours, Mum.'

Mrs Noriega waved a hand. 'I'm not interested in jewellery, especially not when it will also be a good source of capital in times of need.' She smiled wryly. 'Or you could give it to your future wife.'

'Let's go downstairs and open a bottle of champagne!' Eduardo said, and he threw his arm around Claire's shoulders and led the way.

The two women followed and he left them in the hall while he went to get a bottle from the cellar. Sophia Noriega put on her glasses and unrolled the papers. After a few seconds, her hand flew to her mouth.

'Maria! Do you know what this is?'

Maria didn't say anything, but Claire could tell she was on the brink of asking how she was supposed to know.

Eduardo returned with a bottle in his hand and Sophia handed the papers to him wordlessly. He put the bottle on a nearby table and Maria bustled towards a nearby cupboard to get some glasses.

Eduardo read and uttered, 'Good God!' Claire was curious but waited silently until he continued with, 'Maria, you know how you're illegitimate?'

Maria straightened and turned to him with a look like thunder. 'I was never allowed to forget it.'

'Do you know the name of your father?'

'No, my mother never told me, she never told anyone as far as I know. She died taking the name with her to her grave. What's this all about?'

Eduardo lifted the papers and jiggled them around. 'This is your birth certificate, Maria. You are the daughter of Antonio De Silva — Philip's father. Philip is your half-brother!'

Maria dropped into the nearest chair, the colour draining from her face, her hand fluttering at her throat. 'Don't be so silly . . . '

Eduardo held out the papers in her direction. 'Read for yourself, Maria. Antonio De Silva was your father and before he died, he had the decency to leave you half the farm. There's his handwritten will saying so.'

With a shocked expression, Maria stammered, 'Why were the papers hidden in your grandparents' furniture?'

Eduardo shrugged. 'Who knows?

Perhaps before he died Antonio De Silva told my grandparents to tell Maria the truth, and they never did.'

'Your grandmother was determined that I should come here and work for her, though I never really understood why. If she hadn't persuaded my mother to let me go, I would never have left the village.'

Sophia said, 'Perhaps my mother found the truth out accidentally and wanted to do what they could for you under the circumstances. I remember my father saying Antonio De Silva drank a lot and perhaps he let something slip when he was drunk. He was a very harsh, aggressive and unforgiving man,' she recalled. 'You must have been born when he was a young man, Maria, and he didn't marry Philip's mother until he was in his thirties.

'He may have put pressure on my parents not to reveal anything until after his death because of the scandal it would cause, and when he died they were probably panicky and didn't know what to do for the best because Philip was a good friend. They put off telling anyone — and then it was too late.'

Sophia put an arm across her friend's shoulder. 'It wasn't fair, but it was a different world in those days. We can only guess why they kept it secret.'

Eduardo declared, 'Well — times have changed and Maria is entitled to half the farm. This document says so.'

Maria waved her hands nervously. 'Who needs half a farm?'

Eduardo knelt in front of her. 'Maria, Philip is your half-brother and I know how much you have always liked each other.' Maria nodded. 'Perhaps some instinct guided you. Don't you want him to know you're his sister?'

'But it will cause resentment. If I own half of the farm, I can give my share to whoever I like, can't I?'

Eduardo nodded.

'Elena and Juan are entitled to their father's share, but if I can dispose of the other half as I like, who else would I give it to, but you? You drive me mad sometimes, but I love you as if you were my own.'

There was a moment's silence, and Claire noticed Sophia Noriega had tears in her eyes. Even as an outsider, Claire felt the same way.

Eduardo hugged the old woman. 'Let's take things one at a time. First we're going to have a glass of champagne to celebrate. We both have something to celebrate.'

He smiled broadly. 'Then I'm going to check the legalities and when I come back, you're going to put on your best frock and we'll both pay Philip a visit and explain things. It'll be a shock, no doubt, but he has a right to know. It will depend on how he reacts as to how things will go from then on.'

'You'll come with me?' Maria asked nervously.

'Of course I will.'

Maria nodded. She was still dazed, but Claire could tell that she was gradually absorbing the news and thinking about the consequences.

Claire felt delighted for them all, but especially for Eduardo. The find of the coins and the jewellery would take a lot of pressure off him. He filled long-stemmed crystal glasses and handed them around.

Eduardo lifted his glass. 'Here's to us — and the future.'

They all echoed, 'To the future . . . '

Claire commented, 'Your grandfather chose a fantastic hiding place. I wonder how they got at it? And why didn't your grandmother tell you about it and what they'd hidden in there before she died?'

Eduardo took a sip and said, 'I presume my grandparents edged it away from the wall whenever they needed to get at the hiding place. It would have been easier to get at it from the back than trying to reach it from the front.

'As to why my grandmother never told us . . . she died unexpectedly. She suffered a stroke and only regained consciousness for a short time. She couldn't speak but she did scribble 'furniture' on a piece of paper.

'We all thought that she was reminding us not to let the furniture go, didn't we, Mum?'

Sophia nodded. 'We never imagined it was anything of special significance.'

Maria stood clasping her glass and beaming at them all.

Eduardo looked at Claire. 'And we have Claire to thank for it. This will change a lot of things for us all, you know.'

Claire waved her hand dismissively. 'I only found what was already there. Any other restorer would have found it.'

They began to examine the jewellery. The various pieces were in old-fashioned settings but the items were obviously of high quality; necklaces, bracelets, earrings, brooches, and a couple of spectacular rings.

Eduardo watched the women indulgently as they commented excitedly and examined it all.

Maria picked up a square-cut emerald ring. 'I'd forgotten all about this. It was Señora Noriega's engagement ring. I can't remember when she stopped wearing it, but I can remember she did wear it all the time when I first came here to work.'

There was an animated and spirited atmosphere, and Claire withdrew silently as soon as she had a chance to leave them to their discussion of their good luck among themselves.

She didn't intend to carry on with the work today, so she left them to it and went for a walk.

She met the children playing badminton nearby and they all decided to go to the pond to practise skimming stones again.

* * *

When she went to the main house for the evening meal, she was curious about Maria's confrontation with Philip De Silva. Maria was bustling about as busy as ever, but she was beaming.

Claire glanced eagerly from Eduardo

to Sophia Noriega and asked, 'And? Tell me what happened, then!'

It was Eduardo who replied, 'Philip was shocked, but he has always been a fair man. After a little time to take the situation in, he hugged his half-sister and welcomed her to the family.'

'Whew! That's good — and a very generous reaction, considering what the financial consequences are.'

Eduardo nodded. 'Philip was okay. It was only when he called Elena and Juan in that the conflict developed. They were very shocked. Juan threatened Maria and said he would contest the will. When I said that I'd already checked the legalities he nearly blew a blood vessel. Elena was not quite so antagonistic but she clearly wasn't happy either.

'Then our Maria took the stage,' he said with a broad grin. 'Go on — tell them what you said, Maria.'

Enthusiastically waving a serving spoon, Maria announced, 'I told the two of them that they should either pull up their socks and do something to help their father on the farm, or they should look for somewhere else to live, that's what I said!'

Sophia said, 'Good for you!'

'Elena was so depressed that she'd only inherit a quarter, she didn't protest much,' Maria added. 'By the time we left, she'd agreed to do the office work and organise the house. Up till now Philip had been doing the clerical work on top of everything else and Jacinta was responsible for everything to do with the house. The two of them were living off the effort of other people and I told them it had to stop. I think Philip was glad that someone was pressuring them at last, he didn't protest and didn't object. That's why Elena gave in so easily.'

Claire asked, 'And Juan?'

'Juan stormed off, telling me that he didn't intend to take orders from a servant, I told him to pack his bags — and not to take anything that didn't belong to him.'

Claire laughed. 'Oh, dear! Where will he go?'

Maria shrugged. 'I don't know and I don't care. He's never done a thing to help his father, and he'll never change his ways. But enough of this; our food is getting cold.'

Everyone was in high spirits and there was a bottle of extra-good wine on the table. Claire wondered if Maria had thought it all through yet. She didn't need to stay and doing the cooking any more.

They all lingered around the table longer than usual and towards the end of the evening, Eduardo said, 'I'm going to take one of the gold coins with me tomorrow. After I've settled the deal with the farmer, I'll carry on and visit Javier Gomez in Zaragoza. Do you remember him, Mother? He went into banking when we finished university. He'll be able to help identify the value and advise me what I should do.'

Claire tipped her head to the side. 'And are you still hoping to make a deal with the farmer? Push the price down?'

He grinned. 'Of course! A farmer is a farmer!'

* * *

Next morning Eduardo had already left before she went across to the house. Maria tried to persuade her to drink another coffee but Claire managed to escape and went upstairs to finish the wardrobe.

Everything was as she'd left it. The morning passed quickly and the repaired leg was soon fixed in position. The glue still had to harden, but by the time Eduardo returned, they would be able to raise the wardrobe again, and it would stand in its former position.

She wondered if anyone would ever use the secret compartment again. It had probably been there since the wardrobe was made. She heard the children return home from school and she left by the main entrance, so as not to disturb their lunchtime.

Back at the cottage, she suddenly realised that her work was now officially finished. She'd completed everything she'd come to repair and everything had worked out beautifully. She was pleased and proud that she'd given the pieces of furniture a new lease of life.

She spent the afternoon cleaning and repacking all her tools and equipment. The Jeep looked a lot emptier now than when she'd arrived; then it had contained pieces of spare wood, glass, things for cleaning and polishing and boxes of other items like strainers, strippers, rags, abrasives and sanding paper — all used up now.

She sat outside the cottage and mused that this could be her last evening here. Eduardo would be back tomorrow, and once she'd taken leave of him and given him the final bill, there was nothing to keep her at Casona de la Esquina any more.

She slept badly that night.

* * *

Next morning she spent a lot of time cleaning the cottage before she left, so that she would save Maria the bother. She even washed the Jeep for lack of something else to do.

When she met Alisa in the afternoon she was glad to suggest they could visit the duck pond together — Alisa was always in favour of that. Antonio was busy with a project he was doing for the school.

They set off at a dawdling pace and Alisa chattered to her about her teacher at school and all about her best friend there. Claire mused that it was a pity the children were never in one place long enough to make real friends. Perhaps that wouldn't matter so much when they were older, but at their age it was important for children to have continuity in their lives.

When they reached the pond, Alisa began to call her duck, and it actually appeared out of the reeds where it had probably been having an afternoon siesta. Claire left Alisa chatting to the duck and feeding it some of the biscuits she had in her pocket.

She climbed the incline to take one last look at Eduardo's grandmother's cottage and was surprised to see smoke coming out of the chimney — as if someone was there. Looking more closely, she saw that the door was standing open.

She couldn't take the chance of investigating. It could be a tramp; someone who wouldn't hesitate to get violent if she tried to interfere. She also had Alisa with her and she didn't intend to involve her in any danger.

Claire ran helter-skelter down the slope and back to Alisa. 'We have to go back, Alisa. I've forgotten something important.'

'Oh, Claire! I haven't finished feeding him yet. Look, he's still hungry.'

Claire didn't dare say that as ducks went he was fat, so she continued to persuade Alisa by saying, 'I know, but you can come back later. I'll come with you if I can. He's had some biscuits so he's not starving. Besides, ducks are not supposed to eat biscuits; they're supposed to eat green stuff. If you go on feeding him bread and biscuits he'll end up sick,' she pleaded. 'Please Alisa, it's important that we go now.'

Alisa said grudgingly, 'Oh, all right!' She got up and brushed the crumbs from her skirt. The other ducks gathered greedily.

Claire set off, trying not to be too impatient. Without Alisa she would have made faster progress, but they were still hurrying. Coming within sight of the farmhouse, she felt a surge of relief to see Eduardo's car and Eduardo within sight, getting something out of the boot.

She shouted to him, 'Eduardo!' He looked up and smiled.

Claire's heart fluttered and when she reached him, the world stood still. It had only been a day, but until now she didn't realise how much she had missed him. They faced one another silently and smiled in earnest. Claire remembered why she was here when Alisa grabbed his hand and he swung her up onto his shoulder.

'Where have you two been? Out to see that infernal duck again, no doubt?'

Pouting, Alisa said firmly. 'He is not an infernal duck, he's my duck, actually.'

Eduardo nodded seriously.

Claire didn't give him chance to say more. 'Eduardo, there's something strange going on at your grandmother's cottage. Smoke is coming out of the chimney and the door is open.'

Puzzlement spread across his face. 'Smoke? Really? I'd better go and check it out.'

She nodded. 'I didn't want to take the chance of going there on my own, especially with Alisa. I came back to find Pablo.'

'Good thing you didn't try anything. It could be kids messing around, I suppose, but I'll go and find out.'

He set off in the direction she'd come from with long purposeful strides. She followed automatically. He was soon a long way ahead of her, and as Alisa was with her too, there was no chance of Claire catching up. On the way Alisa picked up a stone in her sandal and they had to stop to remove it. There was no sign of Eduardo any more.

Taking Alisa by the hand she moved on, looking in the direction of the cottage. The billows of smoke had intensified and there was a smell of burning in the air.

On impulse she went down on her knees in front of the child and said, 'Alisa, do you think you can run back to the house on your own? I think the cottage must be on fire. Find your gran or Maria, or Pablo and tell them what's happening. We need the fire brigade or some kind of help. Tell them that Eduardo has gone to look, and that I'm going after him. Can you remember that? You know the cottage, the one we went in together when we were out walking with your uncle?'

Alisa nodded solemnly. 'I'll run as fast as I can.'

'That's a good girl.'

Claire waited for a moment and watched Alisa set off, springing along at a fast pace in the direction of the farm, then she turned and hurried on, climbing the hill and then pausing to study the scene below.

Flames were leaping out from some of the windows, and there was no sign of Eduardo or anyone else. Sheer fright swept through her as she dashed down the hillside and fought her way through the long grass towards the building.

The air was thick with the biting smoke and after checking again for any sign of Eduardo in the vicinity, she approached the cottage from the other side where the flames were not raging so strongly and she could look through a window.

There, sprawled on the floor, was the figure of Eduardo.

Panic such as she'd never known before engulfed her. She gasped in fright. Tearing towards the nearby door, she pulled desperately at it to no avail; it was locked.

Running her hands through her hair, she tried to think logically. The fire was still raging within; it was only a question of time before the supporting beams everywhere would be on fire and the whole building would collapse. Inside, the smoke would be overpowering and unbearable.

She ran to peer in at his figure on the floor once again. She shouted and shouted, but there was no reaction, no movement.

She had to do something.

Looking round desperately she searched for something to lever the door away and found nothing.

The windows were barred. Her panic grew by the second. Her glance drifted across the old flowerbed and she thought of his grandmother — oh, she had always kept a spare key under the nearby boulder, Eduardo had mentioned that!

Praying that it was still there she ran

and pushed it aside. Relief flooded her as she grabbed the rusty key.

Fumbling with the lock, she finally managed to open the door and the heat hit her in the face as she headed towards Eduardo. Behind him, the flames were already licking at the door and some of the beams.

The smoke was thick and acrid. Claire began to cough and her eyes streamed.

She had to get him out as fast as she could and there was only one way; she had to drag him. She grabbed him under his armpits and pulled.

He was heavy, much heavier than she expected, and she made slow progress. She gasped for breath, and as she glanced behind her for the way out she was rewarded with a lungful of smoke. At last she was in sight of the doorway, and that gave her the strength to pull him the last couple of yards, past the doorway and a little away from the burning cottage, where she collapsed, exhausted and coughing.

Eduardo was still breathing, but his pulse was weak and he was still unconscious. Struggling to her feet, Claire knew she had to pull him further away from danger. They were too close to the building.

She hauled him along for a while and until they were facing the wind. She felt the benefit of fresher air, and hoped that he would too. Kneeling beside him, she took his head in her hands and was shocked to find his hair covered in blood. Something — or someone — had caused him a head injury.

Claire bit back the tears. Cradling his head in her lap, she looked around in sheer desperation.

She had never felt more grateful than when she saw people hurrying down the slope towards them. She recognised Pablo, and there were some uniformed men with him. Someone was talking rapidly into a walkie-talkie.

When they reached her, she felt exhausted enough to let someone else take charge. She sat at the side like a lifeless doll and watched as they examined Eduardo, then carried him further up the incline away from the cottage.

No one paid any attention to the cottage. The flames would finish off what was left.

Pablo came and helped her to her feet. With his arm around her shoulder, he supported her and they went towards the other people gathering around Eduardo. The noise of a helicopter cut out any other sound. The rotating blades sent the long grass into protesting waves as it descended nearby.

Claire watched through tear-filled eyes as the medical team came with a stretcher, made a brief examination and then carried him back to the helicopter. It took off again in a matter of seconds.

Claire watched until it was just a dot on the horizon and she was left with a feeling of unreality and a fear that he might have injuries that were life-threatening.

The men evidently thought she was crying because of shock, but she was crying for her beloved Eduardo.

She didn't remember much about returning to the farmhouse. Her legs seemed to be made of rubber and she felt weak and exhausted. Pablo helped her along and they trailed after the men in uniform.

When they reached the farm, Claire vaguely noted that Mrs Noriega and Maria were in the car, driving away at speed.

Claire understood when Pablo tried to explain that Sophia and Maria were going to the hospital. She nodded, and had the presence of mind to ask about Alisa and Antonio. He reassured her by pointing to himself. Claire understood that he and his wife would look after them. She was glad. She had grown very fond of the children, but at that moment she was scarcely able to take care of herself.

She parted from Pablo and went upstairs when she reached the cottage;

straight to the bathroom. When she looked in the mirror, she saw how dirty she was, and she could smell the acrid smoke on her clothes and her hair. She didn't recognise herself.

Almost too weary to bother, she bathed and washed her hair and, feeling much better, decided to lie down on her bed for a couple of minutes. In next to no time, she was asleep.

Daylight was fading when she woke to the sound of someone knocking on the door. Dressing in her cotton wrap-around, she hurried downstairs and to the door; it was Sophia Noriega.

'Claire! How can I ever thank you for saving Eduardo?' She reached forward and hugged her, kissing her cheek.

'Is he . . . is he all right?'

Eyes filled with tears of relief, Sophia nodded. 'He's suffered from smoke inhalation and he has a bad concussion. They're keeping him in for a couple of days.'

The relief was almost too much and

Claire had to hold on to the door frame. 'Will you come in? Do they know what caused the head injury?'

'They're not certain because Eduardo is still woozy and he couldn't help much. They're going to talk to him again tomorrow. I won't come in now, dear; I'm on my way to Pablo to fetch the children.'

Claire nodded and looked distractedly beyond Eduardo's mother at the fading light over the yard. 'Don't bother with a meal this evening. I'll make myself a sandwich if I get hungry.'

'Are you sure? I must admit Maria looks worn out and neither of us are very hungry at the moment.'

Claire shook her head. 'Honestly. I'm fine, please don't worry about me.'

'Are you all right? The police told me how you dragged him out. You must have breathed in a lot of smoke, too.'

'I'm fine.' Claire fingered the edge of the bathrobe. 'I've had a bath and slept a bit.'

'I shudder to think what could have

happened if you hadn't acted so bravely,' Sophia said emphatically, pressing her hand over Claire's.

Claire smiled weakly. 'It was sheer instinct, really. I hope the news about Eduardo is good tomorrow.'

Sophia nodded. 'So do I. Sleep well, Claire.'

11

Somehow, Claire managed to get through the next morning. Sophia left for the hospital soon after breakfast and Claire had nothing to do but to wait for her return. She gave the barn a thorough clean-out; it kept her busy and occupied.

When she heard Sophia's car, she had to stop herself from running out and managed to wait a while before going into the kitchen quite casually. Maria looked up.

'He's better today. He has a bad headache and he's under observation. He wanted to come home but he's agreed to wait another day or two.'

Maria smiled and Claire felt a powerful surge of relief wash over her. She hoped it didn't show. 'That's good news.'

Maria looked at her shrewdly. 'He's

not allowed visitors. Just Mrs Noriega today. It may be possible tomorrow if he continues to improve. Come on, sit down and have a cup of coffee. You look washed out.'

'I am.' She pulled out a chair and sat down as Maria busied herself. 'Have . . . have you seen Eduardo?' Claire asked tentatively.

'No, no one has. Just next of kin so far.'

Claire nodded, and gratefully accepted a large mug of strong, hot coffee.

Maria said, 'The police just went out to the cottage to look around. Perhaps they'll want to talk to you later.'

'That's fine, if someone will translate for me.' She had to swallow a big gulp of coffee when she thought about how she would manage without Eduardo, who had been her devoted translator since her arrival.

* * *

Claire wished she had something to do to pass the time. She wanted to see Eduardo one more time before she left.

She'd told the police as much as she could about the day before, with Maria's help. Sophia went to the hospital again that afternoon, Maria went to visit Philip, and Claire went for a long walk to clear her head.

That evening at the family meal, the empty chair across the table was a painful reminder of Eduardo's absence. Claire wasn't hungry but she managed to eat a little of what Maria had made.

Before she could ask, Sophia Noriega said, 'Eduardo is much better and the doctors confirm he'll be able to come home in a couple of days.' She looked intently at Claire. 'He wants to see you, dear. They said you can go in tomorrow afternoon, if you like.'

Claire glanced down so as not to show her elation. Looking up, she said, 'Yes, I'd like to see him before I leave. Where's the hospital?'

Her GPS took her to the right

address. Sophia had explained that if she went into the hospital through the main entrance, she would find him on the second floor, in room number 208.

She had a dictionary in her bag but doubted if she could make anyone understand what she wanted. The lift was busy, so Claire took the stairs, but it wasn't that which made her heart pound. Even if it was a visit to say goodbye, she could cope — if she had the memory of him looking better.

The room was in a long corridor and she passed a nurse who smiled and said something in Spanish to her. Claire smiled back and went on, counting down the door numbers until she reached 208. The door was ajar and Claire was about to knock when she saw Eduardo with a bandage around his head, lying in bed. That was expected — but she wasn't expecting to see Elena sitting on the edge of his bed and Eduardo with his arms around her and holding her tight.

With her hand frozen in mid-air, her

knuckles at the ready to tap the door, Claire's thoughts were in turmoil. She stepped back and slipped silently away. She leaned against the wall further down the corridor and felt the tears falling. She brushed them away quickly when people passed, pulled herself together and lurched her way back to the stairs.

Outside, the fresh air didn't help and she sat motionless in her Jeep for some time, the sight of Elena in his arms burning in her memory.

Claire's brain refused to function properly. She had no reason to suppose that Eduardo had ever felt more than friendship for her, but it hurt dreadfully to see how he and Elena were as one. She ought never to have come to the hospital.

If the fire hadn't happened, she would have been on her way home by now. She sat staring unseeingly out of the windscreen, trying to steady her thoughts until she felt strong enough to think what she should do next.

Tears still stung the back of her eyes and her throat closed up. She had to leave the farm as soon as possible. She turned on the ignition and the engine sprang to life.

* * *

When she got back to the farm, she had a little more time to adjust before dinner, when she told Sophia and Maria that she hadn't been able to find the hospital.

'What a pity. Eduardo was expecting you,' Sophia replied. 'It is a bit confusing in that part of town; there are countless one-way streets. You'll have to come with me tomorrow.'

'He'll be coming home soon. I'll see him then,' Claire responded, adding, 'Before I leave for home.'

'The police were there to talk to him again this morning. Eduardo told me they're searching for Juan De Silva because they found his cell phone in the cottage. It was badly damaged by the fire but they were still able to trace it back to its owner.'

'Juan? Surely they don't think he's responsible?'

Maria put dishes on the table. 'It wouldn't surprise me. Otherwise why was his phone in the cottage? Perhaps he was hiding there and didn't realise who it was when he hit Eduardo over the head.'

'Can Eduardo remember anything?'

Sophia picked up her knife and fork. 'No. He said someone hit him when he opened the door and took a step inside. He didn't see who it was. There was a fire in the grate but the place wasn't on fire.'

'That sounds as if someone set the fire deliberately, after hitting Eduardo unconscious.'

Claire didn't want to spend the evening worrying about Eduardo or brooding about Eduardo and Elena, so she asked if she could stay and watch television with them. The two women were only too pleased, and while

Claire's thoughts still wandered, at least the time passed more easily when she was in company.

* * *

Next morning she got up at daybreak and packed the rest of her things. She'd spent a sleepless night and finally decided she didn't intend to hang around until Eduardo returned.

If Elena and Eduardo were planning their future together, Claire didn't want to be there to witness it.

She tidied the cottage, stripped the bed, packed her suitcase, and collected the last bits and pieces from the bedroom. Once they were stacked away in the Jeep, she was ready to go.

She found Maria in the kitchen, busy as ever. Claire swallowed hard and told her she had decided to leave.

The surprise was obvious on Maria's face; her eyes were wide and round and her mouth fell open. 'Leaving? But you can't leave now; not like that. Eduardo is not home from hospital yet.'

Claire struggled to maintain an even tone. She was very fond of Maria and she would miss her. 'I don't have to be here when Eduardo returns. The work is finished, so there's no real reason for me to stay, is there? I hope that he's fully recovered when he's released, but that could take days and I'm hoping there's work waiting for me when I get home. I have to earn a living . . . '

Maria could sense the despair in the young woman's voice and searched for ways to delay her. 'You haven't been paid yet, have you?'

Claire gave a tremulous smile. 'Eduardo knows my details; he can pay me electronically.'

Maria shook her head. 'Does Mrs Noriega know?'

'No, I'm just going to say goodbye to her and be on my way. I hope that there's room on the ferry this afternoon. Is she around somewhere?'

Disgruntled, Maria said, 'She's out on the terrace, but I don't understand this at all . . . why the rush to go?'

But Claire simply turned and went looking for Sophia, finding her drinking coffee and reading the local paper. She smiled when she saw Claire approaching.

'Good morning, Claire.' She patted the neighbouring chair. 'Share some coffee with me. I love the view from here across the countryside to the mountains, it's quite special, isn't it?'

Claire followed her glance. 'Yes, it's lovely.' She paused. 'Mrs Noriega, I've just come to say goodbye. I'm packed and ready to go. My work is finished and there's no reason for me to hang around any more. Thank you for your hospitality and for all your kindness.'

Sophia looked stunned. 'But my dear, you must wait for Eduardo. I'm positive that he wants to see you. No one expected you to leave the moment you'd finished the furniture, and especially not now, after all this dreadful business with the cottage. Eduardo will want to thank you himself. You must see him before you leave.'

Claire smiled. 'It's very kind, but my shop is waiting and I've been here for several weeks already. I expect my mother is getting anxious.' She gave a shaky laugh. 'I shouldn't say so, but I've really enjoyed being here — it was almost like being on holiday. And I'm so glad that Eduardo is going to be okay.'

Mrs Noriega got up and spoke anxiously. 'I honestly don't know what to say, but I have a feeling that Eduardo is not going to be happy when he gets back and finds you gone.'

Claire shrugged listlessly. After a pause, during which she was fighting for self-control, she said, 'Give him my best wishes, and wish him luck and happiness. He has my bank details and my email address if anything needs to be cleared.'

When she turned towards the door, Sophia followed and they walked together through the kitchen. Claire gave Maria a weak smile. 'I've tidied the cottage, Maria. Give my love to the children when they get home. I'll send them an email once I've settled home again.'

Maria handed her a package. 'Something to eat on the way,' she added. 'And don't forget to come straight back if there is no room on the ferry. Don't waste your money on a fancy hotel.'

Claire clutched the package and then hugged Maria closely. A hot tear rolled down her face as she kissed the older woman on her cheek.

Standing alongside, Sophia took Claire by her shoulders and gave her a kiss too, saying, 'We owe you so much, Claire. I don't like this at all, and I think Eduardo is not going to be pleased.'

Claire turned and hurried out of the kitchen door, the package of food in her hands. She was glad that she was ready and could just fling herself into the driving seat and start the engine. She brushed the tears from her face with the back of her hand and waved to the two women standing in front of the kitchen door. When she looked in the rear mirror, they were still standing there. She sounded the horn and took last glimpses of them and the house until the road curved and they were lost to sight.

A short time later, she drew in to the side of the road and looked back. She could still see the roof of the big farmhouse. Feeling more miserable than she had ever felt in her life, she drove to Santander and was relieved to find she could leave with the next ferry to Portsmouth.

12

Claire lay on her bunk and closed her eyes, feeling utterly miserable. She asked herself whether it would have been more sensible to wait, to say goodbye to Eduardo. Perhaps it would have been easier for her to draw a line under all the emotion if she'd faced him one more time.

Could she have borne the sight of him, of saying goodbye to him, without making a fool of herself? No; as it was, she'd had to pull over and sit and cry because she was leaving Maria and Mrs Noriega — and Eduardo meant a thousand times more to her then even them.

She covered her face with her hands and finally gave way to her tears. She was grateful that she was on her own and most people were still on deck; she could weep aloud. Perhaps it would help. She needed a way of forgetting and moving on.

* * *

She drew into the kerb in front of the shop and sighed gratefully. Nothing had changed.

No, that wasn't true; she'd changed. She'd fallen in love.

Arching her back and flexing her arms and hands, she straightened her shoulders to take the first real step towards building a new life for herself — a new life that didn't contain Eduardo Noriega.

Just that thought made her hesitate for a moment.

The bell over the door tinkled and her mother clattered down the stairs with one of her usual friendly smiles. It widened considerably by the time she rushed forward to give Claire a rib-cracking hug and a kiss.

As ever, her mother was neat and stylish in a pencil skirt and a pale shirt-blouse. She held Claire at arm's length and viewed her daughter's tired face and weary expression.

'You look exhausted, love. Why ever didn't you let me know you were coming home?'

Claire gave a shaky laugh. 'It was a spontaneous decision. I finished the work and I decided it was time to drive off and catch the next ferry. I did think about phoning but I know how you always worry when I make a long journey, so I decided to just drive and come home. I've missed you.'

Her mother gave her another hug. 'And I've missed you, love. Let's have a cup of tea. Are you hungry? I made a quiche yesterday, and there's plenty left.' Mrs Coleman didn't like the hollows under her daughter's eyes or the look on her strained, pale face; she knew this was more than mere travel fatigue.

Despite her despondency, knowing that she'd never see Eduardo again, the knowledge that she was home steadied

Claire and gave her hope that she would be able to make herself a life worth living without him. 'I'm not hungry, but a cup of tea would be just right.'

Mrs Coleman hurried to display the 'closed' sign on the door, and then caught up with her daughter, who was already climbing the stairs.

She didn't like the expression in her daughter's eyes. It had always been difficult to guess what was bothering Claire. Mrs Coleman remembered with anger at the way her former husband had controlled the family. He was responsible for the fact that the children found it difficult to show what they felt. The situation had improved since the divorce, but Claire still found it difficult to bare her soul.

Claire had always been a quiet, caring person, but life with her father had turned her into a reticent, determined character. She deserved a partner who she could rely on, someone who would support and encourage her — not someone in the background who constantly criticised her, as Frank had done. Mrs Coleman suddenly recalled her own news; news that she hoped would please Claire.

She had never expected to tell her daughter that she'd be getting married again, but during the time Claire had been in Spain, she and Bill had grown close.

She'd met Bill before, on her visits to the shop, but seeing him every day had brought them closer than either of them ever imagined. They'd both suffered unhappiness, but they were now coming out of the darkness and facing a rosy future together.

When she heard the news, Claire was delighted for her mum. Bill was a dear, and she already liked him a lot. She could tell when she saw them together that they harmonised beautifully. Even if she felt unhappy about Eduardo, she could still feel happy for her mother.

They had a celebratory meal that evening and she mused that Bill already felt more like the kind of father she'd always wished for, than the one she'd had.

After yet another sleepless night, Claire decided she must fill the gap in her soul — and that work would help to distract her thoughts for a while.

She did the rounds of her usual suppliers and collected a couple of items for the shop that would look good once they were properly repaired.

She checked her bank account. Eduardo hadn't yet transferred his payment for the work, but he probably wasn't out of hospital yet, and it wasn't likely that his first concern would be to settle his account. She was certain he would, as soon as he had time. She'd only left Spain three days ago, and even though her cash reserves were getting dangerously low, she did not intend to get in touch to ask about it.

* * *

A day or two later, an enquiry from a customer about a damaged Victorian writing slope sent Claire out on a visit, and it was getting late by the time she returned. Her mother was intending to leave for home at the weekend and Claire was taking advantage of her presence to find some commissions before then, if she could. Once Mum left, she'd be tied to the shop during business hours.

Parking the Jeep in the narrow space in an alleyway between her shop and the next, she made her way round to the front and found her mother waiting by the open door, looking agitated.

'What's wrong, Mum? You look worried.'

'Claire, there's a man upstairs. He said he wasn't leaving until he's spoken to you. He's very polite, but determined, and I just couldn't turn him away. I think he's that man you went to work for in Spain. Eduardo, I think he said. I made him tea. He's been waiting for a while.'

The breath caught in Claire's lungs. Mrs Coleman noticed how the sparse colour in her daughter's face faded away and returned in a heightened hue. She wondered what was going on. 'Is everything all right? Do you want me to go and get Bill?'

'No, it's all right. I expect he's just come to pay the bill. Don't worry, Mum; he's a very nice person, no harm in him at all.'

'I'll just pop around to Bill's for a couple of minutes then,' Mrs Coleman said. 'Just knock on the wall when he leaves.'

Claire swallowed the lump in her throat and nodded. She waited until her mother turned the corner, went inside, and turned the display sign to 'closed'. Straightening her shoulders and taking a long, deep breath, she walked towards the stairs.

* * *

Eduardo was sitting in one of her small armchairs staring out of the window. He looked too big for the room and his rangy body didn't belong in her low chairs with their floral cushions.

The effect he had on her was shattering, and there was no point in pretending he didn't attract her any more. The couple of days since she last saw him had only intensified her longings. He got up as soon as she came in; his head almost touched the low ceiling.

She drew a steadying breath and managed a wavering smile. 'Eduardo, this is a surprise. Whatever are you doing here? I imagined you were still in hospital. How are you feeling?'

His dark eyes swept over her and he shot back, 'Why aren't you at the farm? Why didn't you wait for me to return? You were supposed to be visiting me in hospital but my mother said you got lost and didn't even try again. That's not like you. Why couldn't you at least have waited until I got home before you suddenly dashed off?'

Startled by his sudden appearance and his demanding questions, she felt out-manoeuvred and struggled for an answer. 'My work was finished. Once the wardrobe was in place again, there was no reason for me to stay. I already knew you were almost recovered before I left.'

She gathered up some magazines from the low table in front of him and put them where they belonged in a desparate bid to distract herself from her own feelings. 'I'm sorry I didn't make it to the hospital, but I got confused by all the one-way streets, and in the end I gave up.'

'All the more reason to wait. I know — and you know — that's not the way you do things, is it, Claire? You're too polite not to take official leave of your employer.' He drew a cheque out of his inner pocket. 'You left without this, too. I discharged myself from the hospital the evening of the day you left. If I didn't know you better, I would say you bolted.'

Claire looked down. 'Don't be silly.' She spotted a tray with tea things. 'Oh good! My mother has made you some tea. Is it still warm?'

His eyes were lethally calm as he said in a quiet voice, 'I did not come here for social pleasantries.'

Floundering a little under his burning gaze, she said, 'I know. You called to pay me, but I only hope you didn't make a special journey and that you have other business in the UK. Especially after someone knocked you senseless a couple of days ago.' She gave a weak laugh. 'It would have been cheaper to send it by post, you know.'

'There is no other reason. You're the only business I have here. Just Claire Coleman.' His eyes studied her reaction.

Flustered and trying to escape his examination, she said in an attempt at firmness, 'Then you've had a wasted journey; an electronic bank transfer would have saved you all this trouble.'

He took a step forward and the nearness of him robbed her of breath. Her pulse was galloping faster by the second. Claire told herself sternly to think about Elena, to keep her reactions in check.

His voice was hoarse. ‘Stop pussy-footing around, Claire. You must know I came after you because I simply can’t live without you any more.’

She looked at him unbelievingly. ‘No, I don’t,’ she breathed.

He reached for her and ran his hands up her arms before he took her into his embrace. ‘I’m in love with you! Surely you realise that?’

Claire wanted to grab the edge of the table to steady herself but she couldn’t because his face was inches from hers and she was imprisoned within his strong farmer’s arms. She didn’t resist because it was all so incredible, so unexpected — and so what she longed for.

His kiss was punishing and challenging; it sent the pit of her stomach into a whirl. Releasing her mouth from his, he looked into her eyes, almost triumphant, before he recaptured her lips.

This time his kiss was tender and as feathery as a summer breeze. It left her burning with desire. Laughing softly, feeling her tremble, he kissed the tip of her nose, then her eyes and then her mouth again.

Something within her demanded more of him but Claire tried desperately to regain her composure. She breathed in a number of shallow, quick gasps before she could gather enough strength to push at his chest and take a step back. Her eyes were troubled and a knot formed in her stomach.

Was it obvious that he was in complete control of her and she had no will of her own? Was he here just to take advantage of the situation? Perhaps Juan wasn't the only Spanish Casanova she'd met.

Yet she wanted to throw caution to the wind. She loved him and wanted to take anything he offered — but she'd gone through too many disappointments not to know that any reckless reaction on her part would probably only make her miserable thereafter.

He leaned forward and reached for her again. Her eyes flashed. 'Eduardo, please don't. This is madness!'

He straightened and his eyes were full of mischief. 'Is it? Then I'm content to be a madman for the rest of my life.'

Claire didn't want to mention the name but she was forced to. 'What about Elena? You shouldn't cheat on her. I won't be a stand-in; some kind of romantic adventure on the side.'

He took one of her hands and although she tried to withdraw it, his pressure increased and she gave up. She didn't want to admit it, but she loved the feeling of warmth and affection.

'Will you explain what you are talking about? You do care, even though you are trying to be elusive. I can tell by your kiss and by what's written in your eyes. What has Elena got to do with this; with us?'

Claire stared at his shirt so that she could avoid his eyes. 'I did come to the hospital that day, and I found your room quite easily. The door was open and you . . . you had Elena in your arms. I had the impression everyone thought you might marry her one day. What I saw just confirmed that my impression was correct.'

He lifted her chin with the crook of his finger, and there was laughter in his eyes when he said, 'And you thought you had interrupted a romantic tryst?' He pulled her to him and hugged her close before he released her again and said, 'You are being very, very silly!'

Claire continued stubbornly, 'I know what I saw. I'm not blind — and I'm not silly either!'

He tilted his head to one side. 'Does that mean, by any chance, that you were jealous? Was that the reason that you got up and ran?' With a deep chuckle he put his arms around her and held her close.

'It sounds boastful but I know that Elena's been hoping I'd ask her to marry her. In her own way, I think she might even love me — as far as Elena can love anyone, that is.'

His hands explored the soft lines of Claire's back, her waist and then her hips. Her own desires growing, she tried in vain to free herself.

'Let me explain — you left before the mystery of fire at the cottage had been cleared up. Apparently, Juan was the culprit. They found his cell phone among the debris, then they found him — and the club he'd used to bash me over the head in the boot of his car. Anyone with an ounce of intelligence would have got rid of that straight away, but he clearly thought no one would ever connect him and the cottage fire.'

Eduardo looked down into Claire's eyes and she melted under his glaze. 'He's under arrest now and awaiting trial. He'll probably end up with a jail sentence, but I couldn't care less. He's a bad character and has been going downhill for some time. I feel sorry for Philip — and I feel sorry for Elena.'

Claire stiffened, and Eduardo tightened his arms around her.

'No wait, I haven't finished . . . Elena may seem heartless at times and she has been spoilt, but she did feel genuinely ashamed about what Juan had done. She came to the hospital to see me and ask for forgiveness — we have grown up together, after all — but there was nothing to forgive, really, it wasn't her fault. You must have turned up just at the moment when she burst into tears and I was trying to comfort her.'

'Is that all you feel for her . . . friendship?'

He laughed softly. 'I swear it! Elena has decided to move to Madrid where she has some relations and hopes to make a new life for herself. Elena is not the type of woman who wants to live under the shadow of her brother's jealous mistake.'

'But how can she leave Philip at a time like this? He must be devastated. I can tell he likes you, and to know that his own son tried to kill you must be awful for him.'

Eduardo nodded. 'Maria has decided to move in with Philip and help him run the farm. We'll miss her, but she's not far away, and I've no doubt she'll go on supplying us with cake and bread. She told me that she's already made a will leaving her share of the De Silva farm to me when she dies.'

'She said as much, the day we found the treasure trove.'

'Yes, and I've suggested that Philip and I combine our resources and farm the two properties together. It will take some of the pressure off him, and if we work together, the local community will have no reason to treat him any differently to how they did before. Philip has always been well liked in the neighbourhood.'

Eduardo stroked one hand through Claire's hair and his eyes softened. 'You see, I didn't think I could offer you the kind of future you deserve, so I kept my distance and wasn't certain about what you felt for me. Then, when those coins and the jewellery turned up, I was all ready to find out where we stood after I got back from Zaragoza. But then things went haywire because of the fire in the cottage.'

He paused and smiled in the way that made Claire's stomach do somersaults. 'Did you know the Orientals believe that if you save someone's life, you are responsible for that person for ever-more? You are now responsible for me, Claire, whether you like it or not.'

There was a lump in her throat.

'I belong to you,' he whispered. 'And I only pray that you can love me as much as I love you. I swear you are the only woman I've ever wanted.'

She gazed at him and nodded, unable to speak.

His wonderful smile unfurled again and when he kissed her Claire melted hopelessly, all her reservations and anxieties vanishing as if they had never been, leaving her free at last to say, 'I love you, too. I can't actually remember the moment when it began . . . maybe in this very shop, that day we first met.

I didn't believe I needed anyone until I met you.'

This wasn't a daydream, it was really happening. Eduardo was here and he loved her. More confident now, she wound her arms inside his jacket and around his back.

His eyes showed his longing, and he cradled her more tightly as he tried to explain. 'I couldn't tell you what I really felt until now — and a while ago, I was afraid I never could. You know I'm responsible for my mother and I thought I'd always be responsible for Maria too. Any money left over had to be split between investments and me. I didn't intend to ask you to share that kind of life, where we'd always be scrimping and saving. That wasn't the kind of life I wanted for you; I wanted you to be free to find something better.'

'You are as silly as me! As if that would make any difference. No one on this earth would be better for me. You've already turned the farm around and put it back on its feet and over time

I know you'll achieve everything you wanted. I'm not someone who needs luxury and pampering, Eduardo, you should know that by now.'

He stroked a stray strand of her hair off her cheek. 'Yes, I could see that, but I couldn't live with the idea of denying you anything. But the gold coins changed all that and I have security at last. We can afford essential machinery for the farm and make faster progress, though most of the money will stay where it is, for a rainy day. I was amazed to find out how much they're worth; they're almost pure gold.'

He lifted Claire from the floor and swung her around exuberantly. 'Oh, Claire! Life will be wonderful for us now, I know it will. Even Maria and my mother have already decided you were perfect for me!'

Her eyes widened. 'They have?'

His voice grew serious. 'Do you think you can come to me, to live in Spain? It's a lot to ask, I know, but I can't transfer the farm.' He paused, anxious.

'What about your work? I know how much you love it . . . '

Claire's face broke into a smile as bright as sunshine. 'Of course I will! You know that I don't want to be anywhere else but where you are!'

But then the practicalities came flooding to the forefront of her mind and she mused, 'It probably means giving up the shop . . . or perhaps I could specialise, travel back and forth with work for people I know . . . ?' She looked a little pensive. 'I'll miss Mum and my friends, but flights are cheap and it's much easier to keep in touch these days than in your grandmother's day.'

Eduardo threw back his head and laughed happily. 'Oh, I do love you! I present you with something that will turn your life upside down, and you hardly bat an eyelid. There will be customers for you in Spain too, if we advertise and look for the right kind of contacts. I'll help.'

Claire's eyes sparkled and she nodded contentedly, knowing that Eduardo valued what she valued and that they would help and encourage each other in the things they both loved.

'Christine and her husband are coming soon,' Eduardo added. 'I hope you'll like each other. The children love you already.' He ran a hand through his thick hair and looked a little disconcerted. 'Heavens! I hope I haven't startled your mother. I was very abrupt when I arrived. My thoughts were busy with how you'd react. I hope she'll understand?'

Claire laughed softly. 'She will when I explain everything.' She suddenly became serious and touched the side of his injured head tenderly. 'Are you really okay?'

Gathering her into his arms once more, he held her securely. 'I'm fine, Claire, really. My mother and Maria have been fussing around me since I left the hospital. As soon as I could get away, I did. I came to look for someone with the skill of a devil and the patience of a saint.'

Claire looked startled and flushed a little. 'Someone like that is impossible to find.'

His voice had a triumphant edge to it. 'No — I've already found you!' he said. 'I only have to teach you a little Spanish so you can get around comfortably on your own, and my life will be perfect.' He drew her close again. 'I just want you to stay here, where you belong, in my arms.'

Claire didn't have the slightest doubt that he was who she belonged with; she already knew she was with the right man, someone she'd been looking for all her life.

She said softly, 'I didn't realise how lonely my life was until I met you, Eduardo. I'm so glad fate brought us together. Tomorrow, next year, or forever will be unthinkably empty and pointless without you.'

And the answer, in his powerful, lingering kiss, told Claire everything she needed to know.

Other titles in the
Linford Romance Library:

SOME EIGHTEEN SUMMERS

Lillie Holland

After eighteen years living a sheltered life as a vicar's daughter in Norfolk, Debbie Meredith takes work as a companion to the wealthy Mrs Caroline Dewbrey in Yorkshire. Travelling by train, she meets the handsome and charming Hugh Stacey. However, before long, Debbie is wondering why Mrs Dewbrey lavishes so much attention on her. And what of her son Alec's stance against her involvement with Hugh? Debbie then finds that she's just a pawn embroiled in a tragic vendetta . . .